Proud to Be:
Writing by
American Warriors
Volume 8

Southeast Missouri State University Press • 2019

Proud to Be: Writing by American Warriors
Volume 8

Edited by James Brubaker

Partners in the Military-Service Literature Series

Proud to Be: Writing by American Warriors, Volume 8
Copyright by Southeast Missouri State University Press.
All rights reserved. Permission to reprint a particular
author's individual work will be granted upon that
author's request to the University Press.

ISBN: 978-1-7320399-6-4

First Published in the United States of America, 2019
Southeast Missouri State University Press
One University Plaza, MS 2650
Cape Girardeau, MO 63701
http://www.semopress.com

Cover photograph: A. Sean Taylor
Cover design: Carrie Walker

Southeast Missouri State University Press, founded in 2001, serves as a first-rate publisher in the region and produces books, *Big Muddy: Journal of the Mississippi River Valley*, *The Cape Rock* poetry journal, and the Faulkner Conference series.

The Missouri Humanities Council is a 501(c)3 non-profit organization that was created in 1971 under authorizing legislation from the U.S. Congress to serve as one of the 56 state and territorial humanities councils that are affiliated with the National Endowment for the Humanities.

Contents

Foreword: Bearing Witness
    Jane Ellen Ibur   9

Award Winning Essays
Kristine Otero
    Broken Ribs *(Winner)*   15
Jessica M Granger
    Hindrance *(Honorable Mention)*   20
Bree Pye
    Like You Mean It *(Honorable Mention)*   25

Additional Essays
Christopher Baumer
    Three Essays   31
Gail Hosking
    Sacrifices Will Have to Be Made   37
Charles Jacobson
    The Trail   39
Gavin Pringle
    Run Silent, Run Deep   44
Sheri McQuiston Anderson
    Atmospheric   50

Award Winning Poetry
Bill Glose
    What the Bomb Wants *(Winner)*   59
Aaron Wallace
    The Blue Angels at Naval Air Station Jacksonville *(Honorable Mention)*   60
Wes Smith
    The Watch *(Honorable Mention)*   61

Additional Poetry
Lisa Stice
    Measures   62
    Got Your Six   63
J. F. Connolly
    The Night We Fell in Love with Diana Ross   64
Jocelyn Corbin
    Another Tour   65
Mary Ellen Talley
    "We're just self-replicating carbon units"   66
    U.S. Navy Haibun   67

Jason Arment
    Reports May Vary   68
    More Than Enough   69
Jay Harden
    The Unknown Hero   70
    The Wrong Way Round   71
Bill Glose
    Shark-Mouthed Skies   72
    Jungle Nights   73
Valerie Young
    IGY6 (I Got Your 6)   74
Ryan Stovall
    Bullet   76
    Two, or More   77
Wes Smith
    First Glimpse   78
Elise Hempel
    The Sign Painter   79
Lindsey J. Medina
    The Cost of War   80
    Friendly Fire   83
Benjamín Naka-Hasebe Kingsley
    Fall   84
Randy Brown
    9 Things Uncle Sam Taught Me   85
Eric Chandler
    Presentiment   86
Jonathan Tennis
    Birth of the Nuclear Age   88
    First Reading   89
Scott Ennis
    Leadership   90
Sarah Colby
    Two Wars Behind Glass   91
Aaron Wallace
    Grub Burger   92
    A Poem to the Tracer Rounds at Rayhana Park   93

Award Winning Photography
Bree Pye
    Sugar Rush *(Winner)*   97
T. S. Johnson
    Day Job *(Honorable Mention)*   98
James Hugo Rifenbark
    Documenting Work on the Saigon River *(Honorable Mention)*   99

Additional Photography
A. Sean Taylor
    Combat Lifesaver Training — 100
    Baghdad Lights — 101
    82nd in Iraq 2015 — 102
Rachael Attanasio
    Echo 232 Tusker Medics' Graduation Ceremony — 103
Joseph S. Pete
    Those Who Served — 104
    Mourners — 105
    The War Correspondent — 106
T. S. Johnson
    Weekend Pass — 107
    Finding Shade — 108
Bree Pye
    Praying Soldier — 109
    Unexpected Playmate — 110

Award Winning Interview
Billie Holladay Skelley
    Keith Eugene Fiscus: A Life of Service — 115

Award Winning Fiction
Robert Morgan Fisher
    Artificial Reef *(Winner)* — 125
Amie Charney
    How to Schedule a Nervous Breakdown *(Honorable Mention)* — 133
William J. Watkins Jr.
    Sacrifice and Service (1941) *(Honorable Mention)* — 136

Additional Fiction
Christopher Farris
    Two Kinds of People — 143
Garlen Wayne Funnell
    How to Become a USMC Selected Toy — 154
Monty Joynes
    No Medals Please — 155
George Uriah
    Cats — 166
Patrick Kelly
    The Measuring of Light — 170
Cindy McDermott
    I Wonder How She's Doing and My Connections — 181

Contributor Bios — 191

Judge Bios — 192

Jane Ellen Ibur,
Saint Louis Poet Laureate—City of St. Louis

Foreword
Bearing Witness

A decade ago a student of mine asked if I'd like to teach creative writing to veterans. I said yes at once because I had never served this group. It took two years to get everything in place, work through the red tape. I wanted to get to know a segment of society I knew nothing about. I write about them here to honor them, to thank them for letting me in, for trying something new. I'm a poet and more comfortable writing poetry than writing an introduction. I'm out of my comfort zone here, but so are my students when they first begin writing with me. I ask them to try poetic forms they've never seen before. I ask them to trust me, to believe I'm safe to confide in, to tell their stories. We become a community—tight, supportive, loving.

I'd been teaching learners from vulnerable communities close to thirty-five years at that point, including twenty-nine years at the county jail on the maximum security floor with men. I'd seen men change dramatically by writing formal poetry. Formal poetry is poems with rules, such as sonnets, villanelles, and terza rimas—and a million more. They follow those rules and end up with a poem that surprises them, and also allows them to write about their demons in little "chunks" rather than taking it on all at once.

Writing about war does not need to be a depressing endeavor. In fact, the demons are being released rather than held inside. It is miraculous to see writers smiling as they write because for once they are in control, shaping the pain, turning it around and showing it from all sides and inside out, instead of having that memory control them in daytime, dreams, or nightmares. We laugh often in class, finding laughter in the midst of horror. Beauty lies in freedom, not in silence. We support each other. We listen. We become friends and family. We develop profound connections with one another, and it's on the strength of these connections and with the blessings of my fellow writers that I'm proud to include a little bit of their stories. Their stories have had a profound effect on me as a civilian, a teacher, and a human.

Something about writing poetry is magical. People visibly change as the healing begins. Therapists are smart to send clients to a creative writing class. Students often come in skeptical. R— came in head bowed, no eye contact with anyone, sat far away from the group, looked dark. She wrote her first day, went home and revised it. She returned, asking shyly for my help. We worked on it together, tightening here, adding more details there. She ended up submitting it to a veterans' contest and winning. She read it out loud at the book's launch and received a lot of love and support. She was surprised. She keeps returning, trying new forms. She's warmer, friendlier, has made friends in class. She smiles, she laughs, her face lights up. Instead of sitting at the end of the table away from everyone, aloof, she sits now in the middle with people on either side of her. She hangs around after class instead of dashing off.

Sometimes vets join the group so visibly broken that others worry they might harm themselves. One said he had lost everything, head down, again no eye contact, anxious, suspicious. This man sat at the first available seat, and even though he was physically in the middle, he was way out of bounds, in a daze. He did what he was told, but he was clearly miserable, disconnected. Like others, he didn't know where else to go, so he kept coming back to class. Gradually he thawed, shoulders dropped. Like others before him, he was less anxious, more relaxed. Now, he smiles, he laughs. Like others before him, he got a nickname given by the group. He's part of the group and he knows it. He's letting us in and he's feeling better.

It's easy to say everyone began in a negative place. This class is for veterans with PTSD and depression. What works is writing and letting go of demons by writing it all down. The second part is that we write together; I often write with them. The last half hour of class we read aloud what we've just written, we give witness to each other's work and the feelings that rise with it. Now we're a community always ready to welcome someone new because we know we can write ourselves free.

I'm different, not a veteran, and I can never truly understand their wounds. I have never been in combat, but I can witness their wounds, hang in there and not look away. As witnesses, we help in the healing process for these veterans.

So many vets, especially but not limited to Vietnam vets, stuffed all the memories down for over forty years, and they were being eaten away inside. One uses every class opportunity to write these secrets he's held onto. His work recently won first place in a national veterans' writing contest. He's not holding back, he's writing his way free and is also able to be present for the others in the group. Now the stories are coming out and he looks lighter, free, with a job to do: let it go on the page.

D— told me he thought the idea of writing poetry was totally bs when his therapist sent him to my writing workshop. He was a sniper in Iraq. For twenty-five years he's been haunted by the lives he's taken. He was angry but he came. Suicide nagged at him. He hung in the middle between life and death. He wrote a poem, and something happened that was magical. He saw that writing poetry could save him, so he began to write every day and he came to two writing workshops a week. He's written well over a thousand poems. He's having fun, and he's willing to try anything new. He's connected. He says PTSD doesn't go away, but he's learning how to live with it and not let it control him. He calls me the demon slayer, but it's not me doing the work. I'm just standing over his shoulder, a witness who won't judge, won't be put off, won't disappear.

One man is legally blind, and when he came to class, I scribed for him, word for word what he said. He, too, needed to tell his stories, he, too, needed someone to listen, to witness.

The goal in writing class is for everyone to find their voice. Some voices write science fiction, some literary stories, some humor, some poetry, but there's room for all these voices, and writing helps put the demons at bay as these women and men find their own voices. I am not giving them a voice, but rather tapping into their suppressed voices with exercises to set them free. Through their writings, I go with them into the trenches, inside the tanks, standing guard in the terrifying dark, trudging with a hundred pounds of gear on my back, and we're all in it together. I go with them as witness, we are witnesses for each other, and that helps set us all free. I can never truly appreciate all their wounds, but I try to give support by being their witness.

Many of my teaching gigs have been funded with mental health grants, since writing is proven to be therapeutic. As someone who lives with the parasitic twin of depression, poetry has saved my life. But I couldn't keep it to myself; I had to share the secret. It's not just the writing that's great; it's writing in a group, sharing these poems with others, seeing them set free. Writing formal poetry adds to this quest for freedom: one focuses on the rules and that focus blocks out the judgmental voice we all have inside that says, *Don't write that down, it's stupid.* I want that voice silenced so the important stuff can rise up to be expressed.

Our community heals itself through writing and sharing with the group, a space free of judgment and aloofness towards the rage and suffering, a space capable of handling the horror of truth. Many of my women and men are publishing their work and winning contests, some in this volume.

I'm no longer a bystander. Watching Ken Burn's documentary on Vietnam helped me to have the slightest tinge of understanding military conflicts. I listen as a witness to the memories they have shared, living memories with them as much as I can. My eyes are open. I see where they've been and where they might be going, the future filled with possibilities. These writings need to be written, shared, and read not by only veterans but civilians as well. I recently remembered a photograph of my uncle in dress whites standing on the deck of the Missouri. Yet we never talked about his service. I also learned my spouse's father and stepfather were both in the army, one in World War II and one in Korea. I remember a photo of her stepdad in his uniform. I've learned he served in combat and was injured. Again we never discussed this, and I think of it as a lost opportunity.

Part of the process of writing includes sharing that writing with others, forging new connections. The reader of this writing sees glimpses of war, humor, inspirational pieces, stories, and essays by and about veterans that can turn all of us into witnesses. Understanding between veterans and civilians brings society closer. Without this platform of veteran voices, experiences are stuffed with damaging outcomes. If we continue asking people to be in the military, in combat, we need to be present with open arms and open minds to send them off and welcome them home, which gives them a sense of place with strong roots and makes us all part of the larger human family.

Sometimes after class I drive into the adjacent military cemetery, so quiet it feels holy. I park and watch as herds of deer eat the flowers from the new graves. I have some moments of peace and contemplation, gratitude for my class, wind down after all the energy in class. Sometimes I write. Sometimes I just sit quietly. I find peace in the midst of suffering, life continuing from death. Life is something we pass on to each other. I'm changed, too. I was raised to objectify war, as we all were, but the truth is nothing like Hollywood war; the wounds, physical and emotional, are real. My awakening to the truth in veterans' voices is a truth we must all wake to; Hollywood war is a fantasy we must wake from, outgrow, and it is my wish that this publication will accomplish this for its readers.

Writing is telling the emotional truth, samples of which are found in this volume in its poetry, stories, essays, and inspirational writing. This eighth volume of *Proud to Be* holds important insights by men and women, many who have been to hell and back. They bring us the gift of their writing.

To all the women and men represented in these pages, I say, "Thank you for your stories, your words, your service. Welcome Home!"

Essays

Essay Winner

Kristine Otero

Broken Ribs

Every breath I sucked into my lungs hurt. It wasn't a matter of if they were broken, but rather how badly they were broken. I made it through the night, waking periodically from choking screams of agony. By some fucking miracle, I wasn't on the road that day. I needed time to figure out a work-around for the pain.

I sat on the porch clutching my broken ribcage with one arm while attempting to smoke. Good God it hurt, but the need to smoke was greater than the need to breathe without screaming. I was convinced that holding my ribs would keep the broken pieces from puncturing my lungs if they were flopping around in there. I realized if I took small shallow breaths of air—or smoke—my eyes wouldn't water. It was almost tolerable.

I figured it would be best if I went to the aid station, since I wasn't on mission. I knew I would have to walk the half mile in full gear. I ran through what I knew about treating broken ribs. As far as I knew, there was little that could be done, my biggest concern being a loose rib stabbing me in the lung. "Fuck it, I'll go," I mumbled to myself as I stood, still holding my ribcage.

Getting myself dressed was a challenge. I couldn't let go of those ribs without an odd settling feeling that they were heavy on my side and dangling. I began to get hysterical at the lunacy of this shit show.

There was nobody near enough to ask for help, and I don't know that I would have. I had to put my hair in a bun, and quickly realized lifting my arms above my head caused an involuntary scream to erupt from my throat. The stretch hurt, the scream hurt.

Good enough, my Kevlar would be on my head. I picked up my flack vest with my left arm and felt the pull on the right side of my body. I set it on the bed and slipped into it. I had knocked the wind out of myself and used the time I couldn't breathe to make it as tight as possible. I couldn't have my already-too-big flack vest flapping against my ribcage for half a mile.

As the ability to take air into my lungs returned, I realized my flack vest served as a great binder for my torso. It was holding me together.

I taped a note on my door that read, "Going to aid station. I broke my fucking ribs."

Stepping down into the river rock, which covered the ground to prevent mud pits when it rained, brought on a new radiating pain.

Every step vibrated up my body and felt like lightning. Another round of hysteria threatened to overtake me. I needed to get to the road, to solid ground. I needed to keep it together.

"This is the stupidest fucking situation, you moron," pep talking myself to keep the giggles away. "Man the fuck up, and walk."

Grunting like a wounded animal, each step was intentional and gentle. By the time I had made it the fifty or so yards to the road, I was sweating. The M16 on my back was inevitably going to bounce against my flack vest, so I flipped her around and carried her.

I could see the aid station like a mirage in the distance, the big green tent obscured by the heat rising off the ground over the field. I had walked that route pre-dawn almost every day. I had walked back through it in the dark on the way home, each of those days. I could make it, but it would be brutal.

"Keep your eyes on the prize, motherfucker," I mumbled. Shallow breath in, and go.

My feet knew the landscape. Each step had already been memorized, just like the sides of the road up and down highway One. All of the gunners knew the roads. We could pick out any new rocks, trash, or fresh dirt that wasn't there the previous day. It was an unspoken part of the job. My eyes would tell my brain there was a possible threat. I would jump on the radio and stop the convoy. It was an unconscious reflexive response. Not every IED is a goat carcass with guts made of wires sitting in the middle of the road. Most aren't.

The changes in the landscape would be subtle. Small mounds of dirt, spaced apart, creating a daisy chain. An old tire haphazardly sitting on the side of the road, the wires hidden. A pothole filled in with dirt, hiding a pressure plate.

This is what I thought about, as I watched the tent through the heat of the morning. I didn't need to watch the ground under me, because nothing ever changed in the field. There wasn't a singular path we had all carved out from walking it every day, but my feet knew it nonetheless.

My unauthorized plastic Barbie watch told me it had taken me an hour to walk what normally took fifteen minutes. I had made it, though.

I had never been to the aid station I passed by every day on my way to the motor pool. Out of breath, needing to sit down, I walked up to a medic who was outside smoking. "I think my ribs are broken," I managed. Words hurt. There was nowhere to sit, nothing to lean against. I planted my feet shoulder width apart to disperse my weight.

He looked irritated and tired. "There's nothing that can be done for broken ribs," he said, as he threw his cigarette into the rocks.

As he turned to go back in, in a huffy panic I said, "Hey I know, but seriously, it hurts to breathe. I just walked like a half mile to get here."

He turned back around and let out a long breath in resignation. "Okay, listen, we have to take a local national to the main gate. We can give you a ride to the hospital—maybe they can do something."

"Thank you," I squeaked.

At my relief, he looked at me and saw me for maybe the first time. I was dripping sweat, and my skin was probably a weird pallor. He walked over to an ambulance that was parked about twenty feet from me, which I hadn't noticed. Opening the back doors, he told me, "Rest in here while we get this guy ready for transport." He turned around and went back in to the tent.

"Oh sweet baby Jesus, I need to sit down," I thought. I had never been in an ambulance, and climbing in was difficult due to my five-foot frame and inability to raise up my arms and put weight on them.

I slid my body into the bed and rolled over onto my knees. I used the bench as support to pull myself up. I didn't give a shit about anything except resting for a moment. I sat on the bench at the very back of the ambulance, because I knew there would be another passenger. My breathing was a mess. I was taking small shallow gulps of air in an attempt to lessen the pain. The physicality of getting into the ambulance took everything out of me.

As I sat there, I worried about the mission. I knew my job wouldn't or couldn't stop because of some broken ribs. I thought about how I would manage, taking into consideration I was able to make it over to the aid station without bleeding to death internally.

I would need someone to help me mount the .50, but standing on the turret wouldn't be difficult. I would manage the charging handle the way I always had, using my foot as leverage. On principle, I couldn't ask for much help from the guys.

I felt better; I knew I could do my job. All I needed was to be patched up by a doctor, who would ease my mind by hopefully telling me my lungs were intact. I needed to smoke—again. As I tried to plan my exit strategy and an easier way to get back into the ambulance, the flap of the aid station tent opened.

A man emerged on crutches. He was a large man wearing a hospital gown. He had made it through the flap of the tent and no further. He needed to rest. He took another step forward, down into the river rock. His left leg above the knee was freshly amputated. The gown was too small for his large frame, and the back, although tied, flapped in the breeze.

He took another step, and two medics came out of the tent behind him. The rocks were too much for him. The crutches were unsteady. The man was exhausted, he was in obvious excruciating pain, he was sweating. He looked around; I knew he was seeking help. One of the medics came around to the front of him and pointed at the ambulance, giving him nonverbal instruction before returning to a conversation with the other medic.

Another step forward, the crutches wobbled. The man looked around again. He was desperate for the medic to understand he couldn't make it through the rocks to the ambulance.

My pain was gone. I stood up, frantic to help him. He needed a voice. "Hey, man! He needs help, he can't walk on those crutches through the rocks," I yelled at the medic. My heart was pounding in my ears. "You need to help him."

The two medics stopped bullshitting and looked up. "We can't help him," the medic who offered the ride told me.

I didn't understand. I wanted an explanation. This man was not in any condition to be moved. This man was basically fucking naked. This man was also a local national who had been caught in the crossfire of a firefight. According to the medics, this man was "lucky" our noble country had Standard Operating Procedures in place which allowed for him to be "saved." They had done what they could and amputated his leg, because it was the easiest thing to do. Recovery time wasn't an amenity the Army offered. As soon as he was awake, he had to be transported to the gate, which was a mile from the main road.

I received all of this information in a very matter of fact way. The medic thought I felt put out by having to ride with him. He was wrong. I was thinking there was no way this man could walk the mile from our guard shack to the road, and then what, hitchhike?

The man made it to the back of the ambulance on his own. Like me, he couldn't figure out how to get in. He was exhausted. He leaned the front of his body against the open bed of the ambulance, setting the crutches off to the side. He lifted the stump as if to climb in, seeming to forget he didn't have a leg. He howled the most gut-wrenching sound I have ever heard in my life. He began to sob. The sutures had torn open under the bandage. The blood soaked through it. He was stuck. He wanted to give up, but there was no place to go. I was trapped in the back of the ambulance. I yelled at the medic again, "Fucking help him."

The man looked at me with tears streaming down his face. He knew the intention of my words. I was frozen; I couldn't even try to help lift him. The thought of going near him, of touching him, seemed impossible, as if one of us was tainted. In some weird way this was my fault. I was responsible for this man's pain and amputation. I was responsible for his fear and helplessness.

This was the war I was fighting in. Every day, those shots we fired hit someone. This was what the aftermath of my actions looked like. I had never had to see this part of it. I had never thought about this part of it. War is about survival, and I had always managed to keep that frame of mind.

On this day, I was forced to see what I had done, what I was doing, what this war truly meant. I was physically sick. I wanted to cry, I wanted to scream, I wanted to beg this man for forgiveness. I was ashamed and horrified.

I jumped out of the ambulance, only a twinge of my own pain registering. The man sat on the bench crying, his hospital gown askew showing his naked body, and his bloody stump now dripping onto the floor.

I ran behind the port-o-potty and threw up, dizzy. Dry heaving with lightning radiating in my ribs. It didn't matter anymore. I wiped my mouth and eyes and came back around to the ambulance. The medics didn't give a shit about the guy's bleeding stump.

I looked at the man, trying to tell him I was sorry without saying anything.

"I'm not going," I told the medic without looking at him as I turned around to walk back.

"We just have to drop him at the gate."

"Fuck you, man," I said as I walked off.

I lit a cigarette and walked back across the field my feet had memorized, silently sobbing. I was in pain, and I now relished every stab, every breath. I had come face to face with the monster I now was. My actions reflected in the crying man's bleeding stump. I knew in that moment if any hell existed, my damned soul would go there when this war killed me. I felt relieved at this understanding; I deserved it. I deserved it for the man who sat bleeding and crying.

As I approached the conexs, I regained my composure. I tucked my self-hatred away. I would do my job, I would fire my .50. Nothing would change. It couldn't. I was a soldier.

Anytime I felt like complaining about not being able to breathe, I thought of the man, and took a deep and intentionally painful breath.

Essay Honorable Mention

Jessica M Granger

Hindrance

The sirens started to melt into one another as multiple fire trucks turned down the street beneath our flat. I opened my eyes. The smoke covered the moon. It was so dark in the room, I was disoriented. I followed the flashing red lights to the windowpane.

Kristy, my new roommate for a study-abroad internship in London, was already in the apartment when I arrived. I was working on my MFA in creative writing at the University of Texas–El Paso. I knocked on our bedroom door and peeked around the jamb with a smile. Kristy and I had taken a few classes online together, and I was excited to finally meet her in person.

"How was your flight?" Kristy asked me as she got up off her bed with a hand out.

"It was good," I laughed and gave her my hand, "but I couldn't sleep much."

I took the overnight flight from New York City to London, England, on June 12. It was mid-day on June 13 by the time I reached our flat in Notting Hill. I was looking forward to going to bed early that night, right after our welcome dinner to meet the undergraduate students we'd be teaching during the twenty-day study-abroad program.

I unpacked after dinner while Kristy and I joked about how small the room we were sharing was. There was about a foot of space between her bed and mine. London was unusually hot and the flat didn't have air conditioning. I kept telling her we sounded super-American bitching about the lack of AC, but the only thing available in the flat to cool us down was a tiny fan you'd find in an office cubicle.

Kristy placed it on my nightstand and pointed it at the two of us as the sun went down. We managed to wrestle open the old window together before bed in an effort to save us from our misery. I gave her a high-five as the window finally stayed in its position, and tucked myself into the thin sheet on my twin-sized mattress.

The smoke reached out first, tumbling into our wide-open window before the alarms could rouse us. One fire truck went by, and I stirred, looked at my cell to see it was 1:30 a.m., but fell back into exhaustion.

An apartment building was on fire up the street. I remember worrying because my program was split up between three different apartment buildings throughout the Notting Hill area. The building engulfed in flames was a high rise, much higher than any of our apartments. I called the program coordinator anyway. His apartment was much closer to the fire. He told me he was recording it on his phone. That people were trapped and screaming for someone to save them.

The sirens wailed well into the morning. I sat up and cried for the many people still inside the building. The fire was still not under control as forty fire trucks took up most of the city streets. My mother called me in a panic when the footage was posted to the news.

I told her I was safe.

Kristy and I walked down to Caffè Nero across from Ladbroke Grove tube station late that afternoon to meet the program for a show. The streets were busy. People were openly crying. There were already photos, plastered by friends and family to the glass of the café, of the occupants missing from Grenfell Tower in the aftermath of the blaze.

I stopped and stared at the photos. There was a young mother in a purple hijab squatting down at the park with her two small children, an elderly man with gray hair that seemed to float above his dark skin, and a teenage girl with my name and long, curly brown hair, all smiling in flashes of white teeth as they posed for pictures taken in happier times. Kristy was calling my name, shaking my arm, and asking if I was okay, but I was gone, back in New York City and standing beside the same type of pictures taped to the chain-link fence around Ground Zero, the thousands of faces hanging precariously on the fence, flapping as if they could blow away at any moment.

I was released from Fort Jackson, South Carolina, to my high school in Union, New Jersey, to finish my senior year of high school, since I opted to use the split-entry program in the Army that allowed seventeen-year-old kids, like me, to join the Army early.

I attended about eighty days of my senior year, excused from school for duty with the National Guard in the aftermath of 9/11. I joined my unit during ceremonies, funerals, parades, ground zero crowd control, and airport patrols, carrying M16A2 rifles as the terror level rose to extraordinary heights in the local airports.

There was an older Italian lady at the gates around Ground Zero with a picture of her son, an employee of the North Tower.

"Have you seen him?" she asked.

"No, ma'am, I haven't," I said.

My boy, he's here, I know it, I can feel it," she said with a mother's intuition.

"No one has been found. I'm sorry." I looked down at my dust covered combat boots.

We could all feel them, the ghosts of this terrible event lingering in the fear of the breadth of devastation. I turned away from the woman in guilt, let one tear roll down my face as I quickly swiped it away. I was a teenager—the events of the state mobilization were forcing me into adulthood in ways I wasn't prepared for.

The fire in Grenfell Tower was said to be the work of a faulty refrigerator. The building had been overhauled earlier in the year, and the new cladding was possibly to blame for the fire spreading so far and fast, the polyethylene of the inside ignited swiftly while the metal of the exterior contained it, pushing the fire back into the building and into the homes of seventy-one occupants who lost their lives.

Even as I am an empathetic person, the thought of dead bodies has become less difficult to handle as my medical career progresses, but I can still remember the first person I ever watched die.

There was a call to arms within two years of the World Trade Center collapsing under the weight of a terrorist act. I was deployed to Kosovo on Christmas Day, 2003. I was stationed in Camp Bondsteel, Kosovo, as part of Task Force Medical Falcon. It was four months into this deployment, in April of 2004, that at least one Jordanian police officer working with the United Nations opened fire on the American police force as they rode out of a prison gate in a multi-passenger van, the cramped space of the van making it impossible to get away as the bullets pierced the metal of the van.

The altercation was perpetrated by the Jordanians after a reported argument about the United States' recent invasion of Iraq.

A mass-casualty alarm rang out through the base that same night. I slung my rifle across my back and ran to the field hospital with my roommate, Traveé, running alongside me. Soldiers were shouting orders, giving a report on a bullhorn that we had several gunshot wound victims landing in a helicopter, ETA six minutes, they shouted, *ballistic trauma incoming.*

I took off my BDU, battle dress uniform, jacket, and put on a green scrub top. I stood in the receiving hallway with the hospital staff and waited for the initial four-man team to run out to the helicopter and rush one of the officers in on a stretcher. I went next, grabbing the foot of a stretcher carrying the body of a man in his early forties. He was bleeding from multiple gunshot wounds to the chest, blood matted in his reddish hair, the dress bandages soaking with crimson blood in the seconds it took us to get him inside and into a makeshift operating room.

I took up space in the corner of the operating room after transferring the patient to the table. The surgeons worked quickly, dissecting down to the bullets and searching for any internal bleeding before they stitched the hole up and moved on to the next one, a nurse rushing in with a cooler of bagged blood, biting the caps off the ends before hooking them up to large bore IVs and squeezing the bags until they ran empty.

I watched as the blood leaked from his wounds faster than it could be infused from a donor. The officer started to pale, the skin bluish and sallow beneath the sharp overhead lights in the room. People were lining up to begin CPR. An alarm squealed, and then his heart stopped and never restarted no matter how hard we pumped his chest.

I went to my office and looked at the clock on my desk, it was 3:36 a.m. I picked up my landline and called Granger, in his room since he was also deployed at the time, his first deployment to Iraq. I cried in his ear, the delay in relay between Army bases so extensive I had stopped crying by the time he asked if I was crying. I told him what happened, what I had seen, that we couldn't save the officer. He just listened.

There is something about my husband that allows him to know what I could never say in words.

He deployed to Serbia on a medical mission in September of 2016. The Ohio National Guard sent their Medical Detachment to work with and allow the Angolan Army to observe the operation of U.S. military medical operations in other countries.

My computer started to ring, offering a green video icon as Granger called me during his nightly routine of checking in. I accepted the call and sat close enough that my whole face filled the screen. His image broke up at first, the pixels of a bad Internet connection shifting slowly. I waited, smiling in anticipation of hearing his unique voice.

"Hey, baby," he said as the connection became fluid, and I noticed he wasn't alone on screen.

"Hey," I said, but didn't offer more.

"These are the Angolans I was telling you about. They wanted to meet you themselves," he said.

I was mortified. My skin felt too small, my face turned red from embarrassment, and it took me a second to recover and greet them in Portuguese. We had spoken about this the previous night. I told him I did not want to meet them. I was sure they were lovely people, but my grandfather was part of the Portuguese Army that kept independence from the Angolan people for a very long time after colonization. I am part of their struggle even if I am not directly culpable.

Granger told me that I was not responsible for the sins of past generations, and deep down I knew that, but I found it difficult to face people who had been through so much because of the country and culture I was born into, took pride in every day.

"Nós ouvimos muito sobre você do seu marido." They said they had heard so much about me.

I responded in kind, told them it was my pleasure, really, to meet them, and not the other way around.

"Por favor," I said in closing, "cuide o meu marido."

It was not lost on me that I had just asked the Angolans to take care of my husband while he was deployed with them, but it was the best response I had in that moment, the repression of apology sitting in the back of my mouth like the burn of bad vodka.

"Esteja salvo," I repeated in English, "stay safe," to Granger and the Angolan soldiers.

The light in their eyes changed from curious to determined with those final words. They gave me crisp nods and stepped back from the confinement of the two-dimensional screen. I watched Granger as he rolled his chair into the middle of the monitor. He wished me good night with a slight tilt to one side of his mouth that said, I told you it would be fine, and said he loved me before disconnecting our call.

The rest of my visit to London was dimmed by the Grenfell Tower fire, the constant reminder of it in the pictures multiplying on the glass of shops, the charred shell of what used to be a happy home, smoking high in the sky, the closing of Ladbroke Grove tube station because of the fear that the building would collapse at any moment and crush us on the underground train.

Kristy and I grew frustrated with the lack of transportation, being forced to Uber if we didn't want to wait for the too-crowded buses. I didn't want to take the bus because the stop was in front of the café, the constant reminder that sadness seemed to follow me like a family member in the faces of the dead, but my students wanted to meet at the café for workshop a few days later. I agreed. I walked up to the café and looked past the photos to my young students seated at a table inside, a sense of hope entering me in the pink glow of life infusing their cheeks as they laughed at a joke I couldn't hear.

Essay Honorable Mention

Bree Pye

Like You Mean It

October 21, 2010—Police Sub Station 16, Kandahar, Afghanistan

It's one o'clock in the afternoon and I'm surrounded by cages full of goats and exotic birds while sitting in the equivalent of a human chicken coop with the Personal Security Detail for Task Force Phoenix. A couple hundred feet away, our Commander and Command Sergeant Major are holding a *shura* with local leaders to discuss all the things we can do for the district over the course of our deployment. Half of those leaders are known supporters of the Taliban. They're probably the reason we've already lost eleven guys in four months.

That's what I'm thinking when I lift my camera up and snap a picture of a young Afghan boy holding a bottle of water to the lips of an older man whose hands are heavily bandaged, most of his left hand missing. *Bomb-builder*, I think, and every soldier here knows it, sits with it, pretends they don't know it, pushes the anger down. My finger freezes mid-click when the man looks directly into my lens, the venom in his eyes so potent it feels like something I need to wash off. I point the camera in the opposite direction, pretend to find something more interesting than a child treating a bomb-builder with bandaged hands like royalty. I squeeze a few panicked clicks for good measure, show him I'm just here to do my job, not afraid at all, even though I'm terrified, have been terrified since my boots hit the tarmac at Kandahar Airfield four months ago.

I let my Nikon D200 fall against the front of my tactical vest, cringing when the metal of the lens cracks against the rear sight of my M4 rifle. To my left someone chuckles, and I turn my head to identify the culprit. No women are allowed in the *shura*, so I've been herded into this livestock cage with strangers to wait things out. I wonder if any of my fellow soldiers are aware of the irony: that these supposedly primitive, weaponless people have caged us, weapons and all, and put us on display for their children. I wonder, not for the first time, if we are exactly where we belong. That's what I'm thinking when I identify the source of the chuckle—Corporal LaMountain, the Personal Security Detail's combat medic and the only other woman on this particular mission. I grin, shrug apologetically, brace myself for the slew of questions I know I'm about to get: Am I a real soldier? Do I actually know how to shoot the rifle that's pinned to my tactical vest by crisscrossed straps of camera equipment—completely inaccessible in the event I need it?

They're a quiet bunch, these soldiers, and I can tell they're not feeling great about spending an entire afternoon with a public affairs specialist they've never met, spiteful that they have to rein in their usual banter. But I've been here so many times it barely feels awkward anymore, so I ask the group of soldiers if they want a photo before they have a chance to do the question asking. That loosens them up a bit. They get up from where they've been sitting on the dirt floor, leaning against the mesh-wired walls, lounging on a worn wooden bench, and assemble into standard group-photo formation: weapons in front, gloved fingers resting on triggers, mouths pushed into serious lines—the tough-guy pose, the one they'll show their college dorm mates and the friends who never made it out of their hometown. I lift my lens up and snap the photo, same photo I've taken of every group I've embedded with on this deployment, then let it fall again.

"Okay, rifles down for this next one, boys," I say, even though LaMountain isn't a guy. "And for fuck's sake—smile like your mama's watching!"

It happens that fast: all four of them start laughing and turn their slings so their rifles rest against their backs. They grab a couple of chairs and put them together, sit down and throw their arms across each other's shoulders, smile like they mean it. I lift my lens and click the shutter a few times, surprised, as always, at how relieved they all seem when someone gives them permission to put the tough soldier act aside for ten seconds and just be human. This is why I'm a public affairs specialist—this exact moment of shared humanity. This is what makes it all worth it.

Twenty minutes later we're seated, facing each other in a circle, sharing stories of hometowns and families and deployment fuck-ups and close calls and lost brothers. Our laughter and shared camaraderie is like a shield between us and this war we're sitting smack dab in the middle of. Our stories reach out like threads, weaving us into a tapestry of memory that will keep us in this moment together for the rest of our lives.

In the middle of our story-telling, a tray of food arrives. Naan, fresh off the bricks from the outdoor oven, circles the silver tray, and piles of challow rice and Kabuli palaw steam up from its center. Resting in between the pieces of naan are tiny green peppers. When I reach for one, LaMountain slaps my hand away by reflex.

"Afghan peppers'll burn your mouth off, Pye!" This from Sergeant Sickels, a big guy.

"Seems story-worthy, a pepper that'll burn your mouth off," I reply. "I gotta see this."

I grab the pepper, offer it to Sickels, who shakes his head and waves me off.

"Fuck that," he says. "Not for a million bucks."

I check my pockets, but all I've got on me are a crumpled up ten and a torn twenty.

"How about thirty?" I ask him, grinning.

"Thirty bucks?" LaMountain pipes up next to me. "Let's see it."

I pull out the money and wave it at her.

She nods, grabs a piece of naan bread in one hand, stands up, reaches for the pepper with her other hand, sticks it in her mouth, and bites off half. She looks around the circle, meeting each of our stares as she chews slowly, trying for all the world to act like this is just a normal pepper, while her eyebrows climb higher and the red works its way up her throat. She opens her mouth, spilling pepper seeds and green pulp out in a stream of saliva, then starts coughing and reaches for a bottle of water before taking a wolfish bite of naan to ease the burn. Even her eyes are red now, and all around her we're booming, our laughter shaking the mesh-wire walls, making the birds squawk and the goats bleat. Lifting my camera, I point it at LaMountain and press my finger down on the shutter. The moment will blur, but I don't care. I pay her anyway.

*

When I got home from Afghanistan I was shocked at how many people asked me what it's like to be in war. I'd give some snarky answer like: "'Bout what you'd expect, I imagine—it sucks. Food's incredible though!" I tried to say it like I meant it—nothing to see here, let's keep the conversation moving. It usually shut them up, but the question rattled through my head and my heart and my life for days and weeks. Years later, it's still rattling.

I'd been out of the Army six years before I figured out I had Post Traumatic Stress Disorder. Six years, and people were still asking me what it was like to be in war. It was getting harder and harder to answer that question, to laugh and give the snarky reply, to make the rattling stop. I finally just started answering with a simple, "I have PTSD is what it's like." Not one of them ever followed up by asking me what it's like to have PTSD—they just apologized, looked ashamed, left me standing there, still rattling, thinking about how those two questions are so fused to my flesh, my heart, my mind, that I don't think I'll ever be able to pull the answers apart.

Digging a hole in quicksand—that's what PTSD is like. It's grabbing a shovel and sticking the blade down into my trauma and scooping out the muck, one shovel-full at a time, only the hole's full of rocks and roots and things shovels can't break through—like Specialist Pedro Millet Meletiche, who died on August 22, 2010, when insurgents attacked his convoy with an improvised explosive device, and I was made to write the first of many press releases for a combat-related death. So I fill that hole back up, move a few feet away, try shoveling out a new spot, one that doesn't hurt so much to dig into. But the more I dig, the more sand rushes in to fill the hole back up, only it's not sand, just memories I can't ever get out from underneath—like the ramp ceremony I covered on August 31, 2010, just nine days after Meletiche died, but this time instead of one casket in the C-130, there're seven. Seven of my brothers, killed on the same day. And I'm trying to be invisible in the corner of the airplane, raising my lens toward the soldiers who are trying their damnedest to walk up that rear cargo ramp and say goodbye to their dead brothers without crying because I'm standing there taking pictures of them on the worst day of their lives—and mine—because that's my job.

This hole isn't going to work either, so I let the sand seep back in and move to another spot, keep digging—even when my hands blister, even when the shovel breaks and I have to jump into the hole and use my fingers, even when I'm so deep that I can't even see the sun above me anymore, can't see the sharp edges of my memories anymore, can't even breathe anymore. I'm clawing through the deep layers of trauma now, the capital *T* layers, and there's no end in sight, despite what my Army-issued therapist tells me every week.

There's no me at the bottom of these holes that isn't always going to have this sand piled on top of her, but because I'm a soldier, have always been a soldier, will always be a soldier, I keep digging like I mean it, keep trying—hoping that eventually I'll poke through the bottom of all this *T*rauma, stick my eye up against that tiny hole, catch a glimpse of Corporal LaMountain chewing on an Afghan pepper on October 21, 2010, myself quaking with laughter beside her, lifting my lens to capture her, and I'll see the whole world held together by the thread of five strangers sharing a moment of joy in the middle of a combat zone in Afghanistan, shaking with humanity—and that's all I'll ever remember when someone asks me what it's like to be in war.

(U.S. Army photos by Sgt. Breanne M. Pye, 1st Brigade Combat Team, 4th Infantry Division, Task Force Raider Public Affairs Specialist)

Christopher Baumer
Three Essays

1. Four Letters

She tells me that I came back different, then her mouth and her teeth and her tongue make the sounds that I already know are coming next. P-T-S-D. Maybe I should talk to someone.

And I want to tell her: Richter came back different. Two months after we were home, at his house—the one that had that fire pit between the main building and the guest place—well, some guy Richter knew pulled out a firecracker, the mortar style that goes aerial. At first, I thought the guy was double fisting, but then I saw that the metal shine from the beer can in his one hand was different than the flashes of light bouncing off the object in his other hand. It was the plastic Saran crap that the tube was wrapped in.

Anyway, we were all cracking beers and talking shit, and this guy lights that mortar and drops it on the ground. When it gets to squealing and screaming, flashes of light blast from the top, lighting up the night sky, pink like a red star cluster. We all get quiet and watch until the lights go out and our eyes can see the stars flickering again. For a second, it looks like a signal flare over the desert, except it doesn't float—it spreads and burns out, fades away.

But Richter's off in the corner of the yard, all by himself, and I can see a beer can on the ground halfway between him and me. He must have dropped it when he made the movement from the fire pit to that shadowed patch of lawn. He's up against a pile of chopped madrone, shaking and breathing like he doesn't know where he is.

That's coming back different.

I don't say that, though. Instead, I ask her: *How? How am I different?*

Short temper, she tells me. *Pissed off all the time.* She says that I'm hyper-vigilant. I can tell that she's been reading the garbage that the Family Readiness Officer hands out, all of those pamphlets filled with buzzwords—*How to Ease Your Service Member Back into the Real World*, shit like that.

She asks me what happened to the fun me, the silly me. The me that shares my feelings. The me that asks about her day and doesn't glaze over when she starts talking, but I'm still stuck on that word. *Feelings.*

And I want to tell her: My feelings work just fine, but Baines—yeah, the same Baines that you've met a dozen times—he might like to hear this lecture. He comes home to an empty house, every single night, with a six pack and drinks each one until he falls asleep in his chair or maybe on his couch. He tries to forget the fact that his house shouldn't be empty, except that his fiancée up and left when he came home, this after a year of shared bank accounts and steady income while he felt the grit of sand between his teeth and wore the same sweat-stained drawers for a fifth and then a sixth day straight. Our convoy was supposed to last a week, but there we were on day 17 sitting in the middle of abso-*fucking*-lutely nowhere, unable to move because there was red air—if we got blown up we couldn't bring in a MEDIVAC because of the shit sand everywhere in that shit country.

What kind of "feelings" do you think he might want to share about a woman who pops smoke once the hazard pay dries up, and now he's got nobody to drink a beer with so he just kills them all himself?

I can't say any of that, though. It doesn't change anything between us, and I know that it's all an avoidance mechanism anyway. I've talked to head doctors before; this stuff's not complicated.

She's staring at me, not talking anymore. I wasn't paying attention. She shakes her head, moves down the hall, and closes the bedroom door behind her. Guess I'm sleeping on the couch.

When I wake up, I'm in the middle of the desert, but I can hear them calling for me. Richter, Baines, all the others. I can't make out any landmarks, but then I see a soft light and I'm in a building and my rifle is missing—*ohmygodwhereismyrifle?*—and a woman is crying so I scan the room and see her in a chair and I haven't seen furniture like this in this country and my wife is sitting in the chair and she's the one crying and I can't hear the others anymore and I'm in my underwear in the living room with my fists clenched.

Where are you? she says. And while she doesn't say them, I hear her mouth and her teeth and her tongue make the sound of those four letters again. P-T-S-D. Through tears she says, *Come back. Please.*

*

I guess I came back in 2012, but it took a few years for me to *feel* back. It took time to shake the feeling that I'm an outsider in my own home or that it's okay to go under an overpass—instead of around it—because there aren't bombs planted in the places that I can't see.

It's been four years now since I came back from the desert, but I came back slowly, in pieces. I was numb for a few years, but then I became a dad and my world filled with color again. I could feel the air enter my lungs and I could taste a Reese's Blizzard from Dairy Queen and I could smell the fresh-cut grass and I could hear that river that I grew up on calling me home.

I'm okay now, I really am. But sometimes at night I catch little movements in my peripheral vision, and when I turn my head there is never anything there but shadows or a little end table or a plastic toy that my son left out. It's these times that I wonder if there's still pieces of me trying to make it back, pieces still roaming the desert. If I close my eyes I can still remember the convoys and the helicopters, our guns and their faces.

2. *The Ground Is Lava*

Sometimes you can see where the bombs are. A stretch of clean earth marred by a manhole-sized patch of dark, overturned dirt means something is buried there. A flash of yellow plastic among the blank slate of brown sand—that's likely a water jug filled with explosives. A wire emerging from the edge of the road, winding back through a sloppy concealment of trash and debris towards the horizon—probably leads to a man with a trigger.

Other times, you can't see where the bombs are, but you can guess well enough to steer clear of certain spots. A stack of rocks on the side of the road tells locals to avoid that place: it's a code saying *Let the U.S. military roll through here first; better yet, avoid it entirely*. A street bazaar—one that is usually buzzing with merchants selling handmade rugs and shiny marble carvings and bootleg DVDs—suddenly feels like a ghost town: that tells you that someone is in the hills with binoculars, waiting for the right moment to press the button on a detonator.

And then there are times when you can't see where the bombs are, and you also miss the indicators. The buried bomb is there long enough that the earth is swept smooth by wind. The yellow jug is on your left while you are scanning to the right. You look directly at the wire and, though your eyes send the message, your brain doesn't receive it; your mind is on your overworked father or your sick brother or your lonely wife.

Because of these misses, vehicles are ripped apart, steel is twisted upon itself. Valuable things are lost: equipment, limbs, lives.

Through trial and error, you learn how men scream.

Sometimes you sit inside of your vehicle for five days straight. You stay there for eight days, ten, twelve. You don't leave your vehicle for two weeks. Everything you do—every thought, every meal, every bodily function—happens right there inside of that confined space. There are others with you in the vehicle, so the first day or two isn't terrible, but by the third or fourth day, you are all out of jokes, all out of stories, all out of patience. You need air.

There is a loophole. You are allowed to exit the vehicle but only by climbing on the outside of it. Your feet cannot touch the ground, which reminds you of that childhood game where you jump from couch to coffee table yelling, *The ground is lava!* This time it's not a game, though. You pull yourself to the roof without putting your feet on the sand, because the only square feet that you are sure are *not* hiding a bomb are the ones where the tires of your vehicle are already touching the ground.

The only reason you choose to go outside is to shit. You squat over a cardboard box lined with a plastic bag and hope that a sniper doesn't kill you with your pants down. You clean yourself with baby wipes. You tie a knot in the plastic bag. You do not toss it on the ground to keep the smell outside; you bring it back inside the vehicle with you. The weight, the impact of your own excrement against the earth, could trigger instant death.

Again: bombs.

Sometimes you sit and study your vehicle. It's called an MRAP, which means that it's a piece of military-grade gear designed to be Mine-Resistant and Ambush-Protected. It looks as though it were inspired by *Transformers*, like it could get up and walk. It's steel-plated with small windows, angular and high off the ground. These features are designed to lessen the impact of explosives. This should comfort you.

Except that it was only a month ago—back in the States, during your pre-deployment training—that you spent an hour watching videos on YouTube that showed these exact vehicles being shredded in a flash of orange light and black smoke. Thousands of pounds of steel, radio equipment, machine guns, rifles, humans, and when the smoke cleared, none of it was left.

Sometimes, while sliding into a dining booth or standing in a grocery store or rolling around on the floor with your son, you remember being in that MRAP. You remember how cold the steel was at night, how exposed you felt in the turret, how the sand just went on and on and on. It was just you, all alone with a handful of your closest friends, waiting for the next explosion. You were on the other side of the world, in the middle of the desert. You were surrounded by bombs.

And you're not supposed to talk about it.

3. What Happens When Nothing Happens

We are told that this story will be about traveling from the southern reaches of the Helmand province to Kajaki Dam. It will be about rolling over 115 miles of road that could burst beneath us at any moment, the weight of our presence possibly triggering a landmine that has lain quietly for who knows how long. We are told there will be explosives in the earth, buried in ruts cut by tire tracks, landmines packed with ball bearings and nails and stones waiting for us to apply pressure. Told this story will be about driving into the desert with our backs towards the safety of a walled-in base, with our faces towards fear. Of what could happen, what might happen. Fear of what we might leave behind or, if we're honest with ourselves, if it might be us that get left behind. Fear of the unknown.

But even before this story begins, we are told that there will be blood. We are told that when we make it to Kajaki Dam, whatever—whoever—is left of us that hasn't been blown up will be met with the spray of AK-47 rounds, with the shriek of rocket-propelled grenades, with the surprise of sniper fire. We are told that in this story, Marines will die.

Then nothing actually happens. The vehicles make it safely to the dam, the only surprise being when Moulazimis drives too near the edge of a wadi, and his trailer wheels catch the edge and slide down the embankment. We post security, then hook a tow strap to the back end of the trailer and yank it back to the road. The sand is soft enough that the tires slide without rolling under. We get lucky: there are no bombs.

None of the vehicles are split by shockwave and shrapnel, forcing us to dismount and load them onto trailers while we sit exposed, waiting to get shot. Nobody gets shot. The *tink tink tink* of small-arms fire never dances across the steel of our trucks. Our daydreams are never broken by the impact of a projectile, a sudden *thump* bathing us in fire and scattering our brains. There is never a moment when a Marine in the turret rag-dolls down into the cab of the truck after a bullet tears through jugular.

Nothing happens. Except that's not really true, is it?

What does happen in this story: we are loaded up with gear meant to last for weeks. The plan is to take Kajaki Dam away from insurgents, to cripple their ability to use it as a place from which they can send small groups south to pepper our bases with mortars and sabotage our roadways with explosives. We are told that this is our biggest mission, our defining moment of the war, the one that we'll tell our grandchildren about.

And then we drive through dirt and sun and heat to arrive at a dam. To arrive at silence.

The stories we'll tell our grandchildren aren't going to be about what happened. They'll be about what we thought would happen, about what it feels like to pack a bag with everything deemed non-essential and then stack that bag with all of the others, a sloppy pyramid of olive drab canvas gone lumpy with our lives. Bags tagged with our kill number, a code made up of initials and identification numbers. We all carry patches with our individual kill numbers stitched in bold brown lettering. By using this number, our mailing addresses can be tracked down.

Our stories will be about photos of our wives and girlfriends tucked into chest pockets, but only after being tucked into plastic bags so that our sweat doesn't ruin them. We'll talk about artifacts and talismans, pendants and colored beads. Bullet shells and guitar picks and coins with our birth year stamped on their faces. Gold crosses and silver shields. Pewter hands clasped in prayer. These things that we kept around our necks or against our wrists. We'll talk about the magic that they carried and the way that, because of them, we avoided touching down on a pressure plate that would take our legs. About the way that they cloaked us in shadow as we moved through the night.

When we tell our stories, they'll be about the leather journals and the folded envelopes and the bundle of pens held together by thin rubber bands, the equipment we use to tell our stories before they're all forgotten. And they'll be about the blank pages that are never filled, that still sit empty on a bookshelf, the moments after we arrive at the dam, after *nothing*, having left us searching for words to describe what we felt. How can we explain that we stared death in the face—how *real* that felt—if death never truly came knocking? If we never really dodged the scythe?

Gail Hosking
Sacrifices Will Have to be Made

For the first seventeen years of my life, I was an army brat. Which is to tell you that the military called me one of their dependents. I went to dependents' schools and dependents' summer camp with young soldiers as our cooks, and the officers' daughters as our counselors. I ate Thanksgiving and Christmas dinners in the Mess Hall and lived in buildings filled with other army families. For several years on a base in Germany we used military script, blue instead of green, which further separated me from the American civilian world. The word *dependent* was written on my ID card that I carried everywhere. Quarter master-borrowed furniture, weapons cleaned at the dining room table, seasons of uniforms, rank-divided housing, and fathers disappearing for maneuvers: it all defined my life.

To be an army brat is to be at home in the world and yet, oddly, never to feel like you fully belong anywhere. It's an obsession with duty, protocol, time, and manners. It's a style of taking everything seriously with encoded messages of *carry on, chin up,* and *police the area.* Phone calls in the middle of the night arrive from the company commander with no explanations, no time for goodbyes. Was it a practice or the real dreaded World War III? It might take days to find out.

To be an army brat is to know war, not because you've been there but because you read the letters arriving from another country you've not heard of before. You see the photographs in your father's albums and listen to the war stories with drunken men around the kitchen table. You feel their intoxicating call to duty with its magnetic pull. At night you cover your head with a pillow while your father threatens to kill himself with one of his military pistols. You hear your mother plead and then your father slam the door, leaving with that pistol. Army brats swallow the shame and silence of the country. They stand with their father in front of the entrance to Dachau only miles from your base. He points to the crematorium, perhaps trying to tell you why he sometimes has to leave for war. Maybe he does this because he knows you might never understand otherwise.

An army brat disguises herself, pretending she is one of you. "We're military," my mother used to say when I didn't want to leave my friends after we received new orders. I say *we* because a soldier's job is the family's job. It's a life of service for everyone in the mix. In other words, we married the military alongside my father, for better or for worse. As the writer Rebecca West once wrote, "All concerns about wives and their children are ultimately deferred to the necessity of making the soldier ready to desert them." What my mother never understood, nor did I for the longest time as I grew up, was that these tours of duty, and my father's future war death would cast long shadows over our lives, even after we left the base.

To be an army brat is to be someone without a voice. One learns early on not to ask for anything or to question the commander's decisions. Still, I was left with memories as a witness in the crosshair between the political and the personal. These memories remain deep in the fascia of my days as I now write about them. And memory, the writer Viet Thanh Nguyen writes, "is a strategic resource in the struggle for power." He referred to nations with that statement, but I read this as the power of my own voice. A voice not included in history books.

This is what I want you to know: war is always fought in two places. And one of those places is a soldier's living room, because war has always been inseparable from home. Try reading some of the letters written by the wives of Civil War soldiers. Or the e-mail messages from soldiers in Iraq or Afghanistan. Ghosts remain even after the soldiers are gone, long after the wife who followed that soldier from base to base is also gone.

Images come to my mind: I am fifteen and living with my grandmother in New Jersey, waiting for the mailman to bring me a letter from my father, slipping in and out of my new high school without mentioning the war, feeling like a stranger in my own country. I speak another language than my civilian friends, with words like *graves registration, personal effects, C-130 transports, PX, battalion, sacrifice, third corp*.

Today even as a grandmother myself now, when the president sends soldiers down to the border or troops off to war again, it's those families, those army brats that I think of. All those empty holidays and school plays. All that loss. Like the time I waited at the Singapore airport, on my way back from Viet Nam with a grassroots organization called *Sons and Daughters in Touch,* and heard President Bush announce on television our conflict with Iraq. "Sacrifices will have to be made," he said as easily as choosing who shall win and who shall lose. With the red earth from places like Bu Dop and Bien Hoa in my backpack, I rolled my eyes and thought of the irony. I thought of what that word *sacrifice* really meant. I thought of the poet Wislawa Szymborska writing in one of her war poems, "Someone, broom in hand, still remembers how it was."

Charles Jacobson
The Trail

> For the times they are a-changin'
> —Bob Dylan

That a dog could undo something that had withstood the draft riots of the Civil War and the resistance to both World Wars, Korea, and Vietnam is patently ridiculous. Yet that's what began to be felt in Charlie Company when Bob took point at 0745 on April 6, 1970, a few miles from the Cambodian border.

After a short while, he walked across an old Armored Personnel Carrier track and emerged onto a single-lane dirt road lined by thick foliage on either side. Footprints in the mud jumped up and hit him between the eyes:

"Fresh NVA slicks!"

Circling overhead in his tiny scout helicopter, Battalion CO Lt. Col. Trobaugh thought he had the ideal LZ for the lift ships to pluck us out of the thick jungle, except for one thing—he had steered us smack onto the Ho Chi Minh Trail!

The squad stopped. The platoon stopped. Bob ushered us back into the safety of the bush.

*

"Capt. Jackson was like our father, to our big family. I don't know—it's just, you get used to ways of one man and then you have to change all over again. I dunno, it's sorta like moving from one house to the other and having a different father. This doesn't work right for a long time." —Sp. 4 John Schultz

Just days before, Capt. Jackson had been relieved by Capt. Al Rice.

The bare stats of Rice were these: twenty-four, ranger, gung-ho martinet, and he'd been acting odd: not stopping soon enough to set up an adequate Night Defensive Position, map reading mistakes—friendly artillery might rain down any minute!

Now why hadn't he told us how close we were to the Trail in the first place?

In short, the seasoned vets of Charlie Company were mighty unsure of their future under Rice. We were used to Capt. Jackson's wise, old ways—no trails. Never! He had learned from a crafty South Vietnamese colonel how the enemy thinks, how to keep your people safe, how to fight the enemy on your terms. Scrupulous, time-tested methods that had served us so well the last five months, here in his own words:

"The people in the company actually realize it that, uh, we take a lot less casualties than other people and they see they see reasons. Like we don't use trails. We try to do things with logic. If you want to find gooks, there's no problem finding 'em. You can just walk right down a trail and you'll eventually find him but it'll be on his terms. So it's just the way we operate that I think is the reason we take fewer casualties than a lot of people. People in the company, I think they realize they have an appreciation for me."

Kay and Clevenger (two of the three CBS TV crew embedded in our unit) got their camera up to speed as Killer (Sgt. Dunnuck) moved up to observe the road for himself:

"Any number of enemy could be lurking behind the thick foliage and trees. The road is only six or seven feet wide, too tight for birds but plenty wide for NVA. Tracks everywhere. Plain as daylight."

While the company waited for further developments, our platoon leader, 2nd Lt. Eggleston, radioed our concerns to Rice, but Rice merely copied Trobaugh,

"Go to the LEFT and walk the company down the road, twelve hundred meters to a possible LZ."

Killer went ballistic.

"A fuckin' road!! Any NVA would be invisible five feet from the road, on either side. We'd never know it. Wipe us all out. Booby traps. We don't take trails, let alone a fuckin' road. It's suicide. Not gonna walk down it. No! That's it."

He took his misgivings back into the bush.

Trobaugh, Rice, and Eggleston—the whole battalion chain of command—were rookies; our company was a walking poison pill. Capt. Jackson isn't here anymore, but his spirit is. We weren't gonna be killed by a bunch of fucking new guys.

To be fair, nobody, including Rice, knew that the clock was ticking on a massive B-52 Arc Light bombing mission scheduled three hundred meters from the LZ. Fifteen hundred meters is the smallest safety margin for Arc Light.

Roll film. Rice came up for a look and to confabulate with Eggleston. As they argued, other platoon leaders and the majority of the company voted to stay put. Rice adopted a different tactic. He squeezed us against the higher-ups: "We're gonna move out on the road. Or I'm gonna take point if I have to. We've got a job to do and we're gonna do it. It's not half as dangerous as some of the crap we've done in the boonies a while ago. At least we can see what we're doin'."

Bull. We'd had Rice for only two days, and today he had chosen a buffet of futility: "Either move out or I'll move out and they can sit on their butt right here. It's that simple. Alright. Let's move out. Make up their mind. Or I'll send some people back for 'em, which won't go over big. What we have here is extremely safe."

Despite him, we stayed our ground in the bush. Rice, for all the praise he lavished on Capt. Jackson, obviously hadn't absorbed his lessons, and he wasn't listening to us, either. He apparently would sacrifice us in order to curry favor with the chiefs. Kay and Clevenger went up and down the column with their camera. Eggleston made a last-ditch attempt to talk sense, but Rice would have none of it; he summoned the dog team and the radio operator.

The dog refused to move!

And so it came to pass that only the poor radio operator—no doubt wondering if this was the last hour of his life—accompanied Rice down the road.

John Laurence of CBS put the mike on Killer:
"What do you think of this operation?"
"It's crazy. It's senseless, walkin' down the road?"
"What's the problem?"
"I don't wanna walk down the road. This is one of the things I told ya about when we were wondering what a new CO was going to be like. This is one of those things you don't want him to be like. Ducks in a shooting gallery. Tracks all up and down this morning. Bad!"

Rice returned after only a few yards. Was he throwing in the towel? No. He made one last try with his elongated southern vowels, "The longer we sit here, the worse it gets."

We still refused to move—Charlie Company had spit the bit. In no time, a cautionary note from Bob had become *Mutiny on the Bounty*.

CBS had their goldmine, a disastrous quarrel.

Then out of the blue, Trobaugh capitulated: "Go a hundred meters to the RIGHT to a notch on the side of the road. Cut an LZ. Get out ASAP."

As far as Killer was concerned, the interview was over.

"Might as well go in and see what happens."

The B-52's were closing in. Charlie Company spread out and edged down the road single-file toward the new objective. The men found the notch on the side of the road and set about hacking out the small trees and brush.

A single chopper squeezed into the roadside clearing as soon as it was wide enough, but it would only carry six GIs. At that rate, it would take over an hour to evacuate the company to Firebase Wood.

Through the magic of radio, Battalion kept in continuous touch with Charlie Company and Arc Light. With two minutes until the bomb bay doors opened, only forty-two troops had been lifted to safety.

"Abort Arc Light!"

"Did you say abort?"

"Roger."

"Mission aborted."

News travels fast, too fast for Lt. Tuck at the battalion information desk. He waited until the next morning to brief the Brigade. That kicked off a sloppy weekend for the army.

The brass panicked. Brigade CO Col. Ochs summoned CBS for a noon meeting in the air-conditioned VIP lounge at Tan Sun Nhut, Saigon. CBS was outnumbered, five to three. Ochs wouldn't let it alone; he forced Laurence to read his script aloud. Every word. He pleaded with Laurence not to release the film. He twisted arms and words, spun and threatened.

Maj. J. D. Coleman, Battalion Public Information Officer warned Laurence, "You better goddamn well keep your heads down."

Laurence was unbowed—his story was already on its way to New York. CBS brass were ecstatic. Walter Cronkite ran the six-minute-and-forty-second bombshell on Monday's April 9 edition of *The CBS Evening News*.

Trobaugh cleaned house in a Gambino-style roll-up. Tuck was banished to a rifle platoon in the field; Rice—who had become infamous at the Ho Chi Minh Trail the same day, one hundred eight years after Grant had become famous at Shiloh—requested reassignment; Eggleston drove a water truck; Killer never got the supply job he coveted.

Within a month, Ochs was relieved of command, a death warrant for his career. Capt. Jackson? Doing fine at his desk in Phuoc Vinh as CO of brigade headquarters company.

As a reward, CBS was expelled from Charlie Company and reassigned elsewhere within the battalion. CBS was only allowed back in the field bugged and accompanied by minders. After their movements had been made difficult, if not impossible, they got the hint and relocated to Cambodia.

When Laurence was scooping the U.S. invasion of Cambodia on May Day, he ran into us again. A month later, he was back at Tan Son Nhut, hospitalized for fever, dehydration, and exhaustion. At the end of June, he was home in Manhattan, frantically editing a one-hour documentary, *The World of Charlie Company*, which ran July 14, opposite the NBC All-Star game.

The mutiny had ended without any killed or wounded and, thanks to CBS, none prosecuted. The collective knowledge of the vets—real people solving real problems in real ways—had kept us safe and out of the stockade.

But the film told more than even CBS knew. This was downright refusal by a crack company of disciplined vets, not a bored, rear echelon bunch of druggies with poor morale! The old army of compliant conscripts was dead. The draft ended in 1973, giving rise to our present all-volunteer army.

> Logic clearly dictates that the needs of the many outweigh the needs of the few.
> —Spock, *Star Trek II: The Wrath of Khan* (1982)

Long live Charlie Company!

Gavin Pringle

Run Silent, Run Deep

The surfacing siren sounded off two long notes, followed closely by an announcement over the 4MC intercom. "Petty Officer Ryan, report to crew's mess. All off duty personnel, report to crew's mess for honors."

Sleepy-eyed submariners stumbled from their racks and out of berthing. The short tunnel running from berthing to crew's mess was quickly congested by men outfitted in identical navy-blue coveralls. As the crew settled down at benches, Ryan was led to the front of the assembly and stood pensively. He was a young kid, fresh out of A-ganger training. He looked disheveled and gangly, his peach-fuzz beard in patches, and his uniform covered in grease, as was common with his rate. His cheeks had sunken in from weight loss during the underway, the crew being on half rations due to the most recent extension. This caused his normally gangly visage to appear more alien than normal.

Senior officers donning freshly pressed uniforms with gilding on their collars soon gathered at the front with clear, bright eyes and comfortable demeanors, as if their racks had not been disturbed by late-night maintenance, and the wardroom had ample provisions. "Petty Officer Ryan has successfully completed all requirements to be recognized as qualifying for Submarines. He has shown able performance in high-stress situations and has adequate knowledge to perform vessel-saving procedures. Make it be known before the assembled, Petty Officer Ryan is qualified for submarine duty," the Executive Officer declared as Ryan's Sea Dad pinned the silver fish on his chest. "Crew dismissed." Rose and the rest of the crew shuffled from the mess with a new brother in their midst. Petty Officer Ryan became one of them that night.

Rose was Ryan's Sea Dad. He was a senior member of Engineering and had sponsored Ryan when he first came aboard. Small, with a thin build and bright red hair that he liked to keep on the shaggy side of regulations, he always seemed to jump at the first available woman who crossed his path. His relationship with his new fiancée was no different. She was a dancer at Club Foxy whom he had impregnated during a previous maintenance period. She seemed like a nice enough girl, but we all had experience with the girls of Club Foxy. Doubts abounded at the legitimacy of his baby, although to my knowledge no one voiced their insensitive opinions with him in the room.

He worked in Chemistry for the Engineering Department. Chemistry was a small division, residing in a small room, beyond the treadmill on Engine Room Upper Level, deep in the bowels of engineering. The room was commonly referred to as the Closet.

Every day on deployment, Chemistry would roll from their coffin-sized racks, stand in line for an opportunity to shovel a hurried meal, take a leak, and head back to the Chemistry Closet. Cranking open the steam-tight door separating aft and forward, they were greeted with the Can Tunnel. The tunnel's floor was packed with a layer of tin cans filled with food for the remaining days of the deployment. A blue mat covered the top of the cans, obscuring them from view. Carefully they would walk through the tunnel, making sure that today would not be the day they'd join the ranks of the unlucky. Several crewmates had twisted or even broken an ankle after stepping on the precarious and ever-changing flooring. The floor could never be trusted; sometimes a favorite supporting can was mysteriously absent after the midday meal.

Rose liked to measure the passage of time on his way to the Closet by the tunnel's headroom. The tunnel was tight at the beggining of an underway, with just enough space to crouch through. At the end, most cans were absent, allowing for an obstacle-free walkway and ample headroom.

With seniority in his division, and expecting the birth of his first child, Rose had put in a leave request for the upcoming deployment. Unfortunately, a few days before send-off, his leave was denied. His entire division was considered essential personnel. He prepared for the second underway of the month the only way possible, with enthusiastic bitching. The crew joined him in grumbling about how they were picking up the slack for the other boats in Guam. Somehow, the *Chicago* was always ready, always willing to pick up an extra underway—crew be damned.

Rose's baby was on its way, but in typical submariner fashion, the needs of the many outweighed the needs of the few. Before and throughout the first leg, it was evident he was not in a good mental state. Missing the birth of his first child had taken its toll. As submariners, we had been trained: "Country first, boat second, crew third." At that moment for Rose, I don't think he could have cared less about the Chinese or Kim Jong-Un. As the expected delivery date crept to the forefront and we had not yet turned for port, Rose neared his breaking point. When eventually the crew was told of an extension, despair consumed him. To be absent for the most basic and intimate of familial duties proved to be too much. Rose broke.

He tried to hang himself that night, rolling from his top rack, naked, the belt from his coveralls tied around his neck and attached to the overhead. The top rack wasn't very high though, probably only eight feet. The Mechanical Division Lead, Smith, found him dangling, legs and limbs thrashing violently. Smith was a mix between an All-American Kid and a surfer from SoCal. Standing six foot and two or three inches, he was tall for a Submariner, with short, cropped brown hair always seeming to be within regulations. Religious about his fitness, he used the exercise equipment strewn throughout the boat during his off time. He maintained a healthy, athletic physique even through periods of short rations, cramming his rack full of protein bars, snacks, and supplements. He lifted Rose's struggling body as he cut the belt loose from the overhead.

Rose was relegated to suicide watch—his belt and shoelaces were taken, and he was barred access to knives. Senior enlisted watched him 24/7. They watched him sleep, eat, and shower. He was taken off duty for the duration of the underway. *I guess he wasn't essential personnel after all.* With sad determination he accepted his fate. He would see his baby, but not as a Navy Submariner. This was the end for Rose; he would never sail again.

The next day in maneuvering, Smith roved in as Engineering Supervisor. Smith was the sailor you always dreamed of being but could never measure up to. He was the boat's diver and was qualified in every supervisory role on board. While most submariners served three and a half years on station, Smith was currently working on his sixth. He had extended his sea tour on the outlandish hope of switching rates, dreaming of becoming a Navy Seal. The sheer length of time aboard made him hard and jaded, lacking empathy toward the lives of his crewmates. Shooting the breeze between rounds, he said, "Rose better be fucking thankful I saved his ass last night. Can you imagine the stand-down we'd get if he would have offed himself? Shit would have been glorious. Might have been long enough for me to go stateside for a while." Although a trip home and a stand-down would have worked wonders for morale, I couldn't help but shake the thought that our friend and long-term crewmember had tried to kill himself. Smith's wife worked at Club Foxy; Smith had even introduced Rose to his fiancée. I believe they had even gone on a few double dates at the beginning of Rose's relationship. Doesn't that sort of relationship count for anything? Perhaps comradery only counted when you could see the sun and feel the breeze. Under the sea, surrounded by darkness and the abyss, perhaps sentiment and brotherhood had no bearing.

Forced to alertness with the constant threat of death, the absence of sunlight playing tricks on your internal clock and body, and the knowledge that the only thing keeping you alive is a hunk of metal the crew lovingly referred to as *the submerged gun-metal dildo*, submariners must make happiness where there is none. They are a different breed of human. They say that only 30 percent of Americans are young, fit, and smart enough to be in the military. The rest of the military doesn't hold a candle to submariners. On Engine Room Lower Level, during after-shift cleanup, I heard a passage from my most recent audiobook, *Call of the Wild* by Jack London.

> He had learned well the law of club and fang, and he never forewent an advantage or drew back from a foe he had started on the way to Death. He had lessoned from Spitz, and from the chief fighting dogs of the police and mail, and knew there was no middle course. He must master or be mastered; while to show mercy was a weakness, mercy did not exist in the primordial life. It was misunderstood for fear, and such misunderstandings made for death. Kill or be killed, eat or be eaten was the law; and this mandate, down out of the depths of Time, he obeyed.

His description, that weakness will be jumped upon, resonated with me. It aptly described my current reality. Crewmembers acted friendly to one another when they postured from strength. Letting your guard down even for a second was a death sentence; the pack will attack you. They will exploit your weakness and take even the slightest modicum of happiness from you. In the submarine fleet, it is common knowledge that once the hatches shut, there is only a finite amount of happiness. To stay sane, you must rip happiness from others. London's Law of Club and Fang eerily paralleled my existence and Rose's fate.

As well as participating in after-shift cleanup, I took part in Reactor Controls Division. A division is meant to be your closest companions on the boat. You perform the same job, maintenance, and are supposed to support each other through an underway. Reactor Controls was the division in charge of Start-Ups, Shutdowns, and Steady State operations for the reactor. Part of our job also entailed doing math and paperwork, ensuring we were complying with safe operations guidelines. Essentially, we were nerds who crunched numbers and kept the boat off Big Navy's watchlist.

Shanafelt, Shanny for short, was a member of RC division and was one of my closest friends in Guam, as well as my eventual roommate. We drove to and from work together most days. One day, at the end of our time on the island, he looked at me and said, "I'm so glad I volunteered for submarines." He quickly clarified, "I'm not saying I enjoyed my time; I just know that life can only go up from here. There isn't a hellhole worse; I bet a Russian prison would be better than life right now."

I couldn't agree more.

Shanny was a kid from Michigan. Tattoos adorned his entire body, both arms had sleeves, and his chest had a raven from collarbone to collarbone and down past his ribs. Along with his penchant for tattoos, he was also a big horndog, always playing the Tinder game when we were ashore. He had a fondness for women, determined to spend most of his nights on land locked in a loving embrace. Questioned about the frequency of his late-night company, he would comment, "I spend month after month in a cold rack, too tight to turn over in while I sleep. Too short to allow an option other than sleeping at an angle, the least I can do during my time topside is fall asleep pressed against a woman, pillowing my head on a set of large breasts."

He started banging this Air Force girl during one of our refitting periods. *I called her Sybil Vane back then because I had just finished Dorian Gray on the last underway, and her name sounded similar.* Sybil was fresh out of boot, with the tight, athletic body of youth. Possessing a heart-shaped face and shoulder-length auburn hair, her presence and appearance emitted an optimistic eagerness, enveloping her in innocent cuteness. Sybil wanted to tour the boat badly; she asked time and time again to take her to the pier and look, but the thought of spending voluntary time on our personal retreat from society was out of the question. Sybil got lucky one Saturday when Shanny got called in to sign some pre-Start-Up paperwork. She had slept over the night before and was up early enough to tag along. "Signing this stuff should take about 30 minutes. Just enough time for you to go aboard and get a quick tour of berthing and the mess," Shanny said as we pulled into pier parking. "Request to come aboard, show your ID, and salute the flag as you walk across the gangway."

Once he had finished up our paperwork, he came back topside looking for her. She was over at the smoke pit, sitting alone and crying. Once she saw us, her crying slowed down, and between sniffles she said, "I can't believe that you serve on that thing; I can't believe that anyone lives like that."

Along with filing pre-Start-up paperwork on our days off, RC division also had Shutdown duty. Essentially, one unlucky soul from RC division and a skeleton crew from Engineering had to guide the reactor to a safe condition, while the rest of the boat got to go topside and enjoy post-deployment food. Along with the celebratory food, topside also meant seeing your wife, fiancée, girlfriend, or kids for the first time in months. Along with Shanny, RC division also included a guy named Mendoza. Mendoza was a quiet guy who didn't like to spend his social time with his coworkers. He was nice enough, but nobody had formed much of a relationship with him, since he was older and had a pregnant wife and a three year old at home. As the lines were tied down to the cleats, word spread that his wife had had her second child, a healthy daughter, a little earlier then expected. The boat had now taken his opportunity to see the birth of both of his children, three anniversaries, his wife's birthdays, and all his son's first three birthday parties. He was anxious to see his daughter, but, unfortunately, he had drawn the short straw. He was performing the Reactor Shutdown. Outside of maneuvering, Mendoza asked Shanafelt to cover for him so he could go hold his baby girl. "Sorry, man," Shanny said, "I made plans for the evening already." On the ride home that evening, Shanny talked on the phone with his newest match on Tinder.

Looks like we're having company.

Sheri McQuiston Anderson

Atmospheric

As I walk slowly down the aisle, my eyes scan each row, seeking an empty seat that might offer elbowroom and a few hours of quiet.

I pause at row 19. I don't know why, except, perhaps, that he sits in the aisle seat, two empty seats beside him, so there will be one seat, unclaimed, between us. He is older. White haired, around my father's age. When I ask him if I can sit there, he stands readily from seat 19D, his legs far too long for me to step around him. I am surprised at how tall and broad he still is. Taller even than my father.

I take my seat in 19F. We sit in silence. After takeoff, I twist my head around as the plane rises, gaze at the ground far below us, growing smaller by the second. It is a thousand shades of green, so different from the lifeless winter brown of my home. The land undulates, parts of it hidden beneath large stands of trees, whole groves, forests, now just a soft bit of moss beneath the silver airplane wing. Waterways twist and turn, snaking their way inland without pattern or reason. My eyes trace their shapes, following the winding lines, wondering if anyone knows the turn is there, if houses are tucked into that forest, if someone beneath their shade is looking up and seeing the bright glint of fuselage pass far above.

Wisps of cirrus clouds waft between the earth and me, tiny crystals somehow forming translucent brushstrokes. They follow me, their drift almost matching our pace as we speed away, leaving the careful lines of this road, this farm, that city far behind us.

Satisfied that we are safely aloft, that all is well, I rummage in my overfilled backpack and tug out a book. I dive back into the story, that of a fellow military wife, different branches, different pilot missions, but same daily realities and quiet fears. On the following flight I'll finish this book, holding myself together nicely until I read the epilogue, in which the author admits that life again fell apart for her once her husband faced a third unexpected deployment. But this flight was pre-epilogue, pre-hot tears that would not stop.

He crouches over his iPad, peering past the glare at black words on a dull grey screen. The steady drone of the engines reminds me of how very late I went to bed the night before, begs my tired eyes to close. Wrestling a small pillow from my backpack, I wedge it around my neck, a meager comfort as I lean my temple against the drawn window shade, warm plastic vibrating the milliseconds as the jets propel us through space, cutting through currents, crossing invisible dotted lines, delineating states that I memorized only in theory as a girl in rural Louisiana who had barely traveled outside a hundred-mile radius. We catapult through the atmosphere, faster than those who first settled this land could have dreamed. Traveling in a day what once took a year. Years. Lifetimes. Simplifying travel while complicating life and love and war.

*

I awake with a start. The window cover of 19F is hot to the touch. Too hot for my head to lean against it. I shove down mild panic. Surely it's nothing. Or my window could be malfunctioning, absorbing the heat from the jet engine that appears almost close enough that I could jump, jump from my seat onto it—if. If this plane were not a metal bullet, if we were not traveling at hundreds of miles per hour, if we were not thousands of feet aloft, if time and space would freeze so I could reach my hand out and feel, feel if it's just from the sunlight, as the flight attendant assures me that it is, and not a malfunction that could shatter my window, exposing me to a rush of depressurization. Yet the rush and thunder never really stop when you most need them to. I wonder if he, in 19D, would grab my feet, would try to keep me from falling. He is still reading. He glances over as I furtively feel the cover of the window, compare it to the milder warmth of the neighboring window shade, lift the shade to feel the translucent plastic of the window.

"It's hot," I say to him. As though I'm a child. As though I haven't flown hundreds of times. As though I'm that girl boarding a plane expectantly for the first time at age twelve.

His eyebrows raise, grey crescents like two birds aloft. "I'd keep my buckle on if I were you," he says with a wry grin. I try to return it, unsure. This is little consolation. He asks the woman in 19A if her row's window is hot, too. She relays the message to 19C, tiny face in a gleaming sari, who smiles, unsure of what is being said, cracks open the window shade to peek at the world below, closes it, and smiles again with a knowing nod, satisfied.

Unwilling to spread my unspoken panic, I sit in mild terror, wondering how much one can brace oneself for a structural failure, or if I'd be better off if I pretend it isn't happening.

"Is Dallas your home?" I ask, trying to distract myself.

No, he is going there to visit his daughter. His granddaughter is turning six.

"Six is a delight." I relax a bit. All is well in this world where little girls twirl and turn six, and grandfathers fly halfway across the continent to witness them spin.

*

He had been a banker in North Carolina. "Are you from Colorado?" he asks.

"No, no," I explain, sure my southern drawl gave that away long before, but playing along as though neither of us noticed.

We moved there for my husband's job as a pilot. He inquires whether he learned to fly in the military.

Yes. Yes he did. He was in the Air Force.

19D leans in, conspiratorially. Suddenly we are not separated by decades and experiences and unknown lives. We are seventeen inches apart, separated only by an unclaimed seat and a hum of jet noise that had almost numbed us into silence.

"I was actually in the Army before I was in banking. I retired as a colonel." It was my turn to raise my eyebrows into a duet of gulls.

And then, "I served in Vietnam."

An inward gasp. That silence can cloak such fierce reality. I offer my thanks, decades too late.

"My wife and I have six children." And then some quieter detail, drowned out by jet noise.

I told him so, that I could barely hear him. He leaned closer, as did I, drawn together by shared stories desperate to be voiced.

"My son was in the Army. He was killed in action in Iraq in 2004."

Silence. My eyes well. "I am so, so very sorry." My apology feels cheap, far less than what his son deserves, than two generations of warriors deserve.

His son's widow raised their three small children to adulthood. His son's son talks about joining the Army. As he speaks above the buzz of engines, 19D's eyes glisten in their crinkled corners, his irises the color of icebergs. I revel with him that his fallen son's eldest son is at college on a football scholarship, in a state where children of fallen soldiers can attend college tuition-free. "He'll end up in the Army if it's where he's meant to be, but for now, he's happy playing football." I think on this "meant to be," and "happy," and wonder how these two intertwine and intersect, never the exact parallel trajectories we expect. And how those eyes, that have seen more than any eyes should see, can still draw tight with joy at a young man's schooling, at a little girl's birthday.

We compare military stations, realize he and my husband were stationed at the same base decades apart, my husband flying the same planes from which he jumped as a paratrooper, from which he'd leaped into the horrors of Vietnam with his men. Generations of soldiers, decade after decade, all jumping in perfect staccatos from an open door over sandy drop zones, parachutes blooming in rapid fire, catching air, their descent slowing to a lazy race to the earth. Deadly poetry held aloft.

That base initiated me into military life. Into helicopters hovering low, blades beating the air into submission, as I drove under their downdraft to the commissary. Into the young wives of enlisted soldiers, digging deep into wallets for enough money to buy groceries as babies cried. Into military towns worn ragged. Into the thunder of artillery practice late into the night. Into the shutter of 9/11 and war and droves of soldiers deployed and the navigation of motherhood, utterly alone. Into bravery when I didn't have it in me, into waiting, into wrestling back fear as I woke and when I went to bed, with almost every choking breath I took in between.

As we unveil bits of our stories, I place my palm on the window shade behind me without even looking. Move it around. Top, bottom, left, right, comparing it to the temperature of the neighboring window, anxious momma taking the temperature of her feverish child, wondering if she should be concerned.

*

As a girl, I would lie in the tall grasses, my sister nearby, seeking out shapes amongst the clouds. We would call out to one another, pointing with small fingers just where the image could be found, hoping the other would see what our own eyes did. "Look! Right over there is the fish's head, and then its tail is swishing over there." "Just over the top of the barn—see the dragon with fire coming out of its mouth?" "It's a huge whale beside that puffy cloud—can't you see it?"

Yet as I grew older, I no longer sought out the shapes. Instead, when I now look to the sky, it's the clouds themselves I seek. I want to read them, to know their secrets. When we lived near the Gulf of Mexico, towers of cumulonimbus would slowly move in from the west over the waves, gorgeous, heaping piles of fluff, cottony white beauty bringing with it violent storms. Small aircraft in their wake would land quickly to avoid the risk of lightning. Baking in the heat of July in California, picnicking with military friends whose home has known years of shared laughter and tears, our children looked up and gasped. Far above, cirrus clouds formed a row of perfect feathers across the sky, magic taking flight. My girls beg for a camera, but the feathers dissolve too quickly for capture. In my home near the mountains, I scan the skies for lenticular clouds, round cloud-orbs far too perfect to be a mere gathering of water vapor. The same rotor systems that buff them smooth and lovely, invisible sky-hands making perfect clay bowls, also create violent wind shear that shakes passing planes and threatens to toss them to earth.

*

Lord Byron wrote it first:

> Sorrow is knowledge: they who know the most
> Must mourn the deepest o'er the fatal truth,
> The Tree of Knowledge is not that of Life

As though he, too, had lived this life, eaten from that tree. Then wondered at his changed self, an orb of cloud buffeted so severely by elements beyond its control that it is almost unrecognizable from its former self, whose identifying feature is how unlike other cloud formations it appears.

I do not know what place I occupy in this world. I have never held a weapon in my hands. I have only stood on the ground, babe on hip, under the shadow of planes overhead, parachutes blossoming to cheers from giddy civilians, unaware that the soldiers dangling beneath were caught in a cycle of constant deployments, wartime to wartime, their families bent low under the struggle. I have never been on a battlefield. My war zone was hauntingly quiet. What I know of this life of service and liberty and sacrifice I know from just one military branch, just one serviceman's job. Yet never again can I be counted a civilian. I have seen and endured far too much for that.

I do not know when the destruction came, when I became broken, whether it was all at once or bit by bit, the slow erosion of all that had been, of all that I'd known. Shared sorrow eroded me, sloughed off my outer self until I barely recognized who remained, this girl left behind to bear the weight of it all. Aware that, around me, a thousand families carried burdens the same as mine, who, too, dreaded the uniformed men on the doorstep bearing words too unthinkable, whose breath caught at news of every airplane crash, the heat and heaviness of knowledge and sorrow, bruising and breaking and weaving our hearts into one. We all waited, tiny town of countless worries and impossible hope encased in row after row of tidy military houses, enacting the everyday while the whole lot of us held our breath, holding sick babes and holding hands and holding it all together as we wondered how it would all end, if it would ever end, if it would destroy us all.

The brokenness left me changed, a transformation so gradual that I was completely unaware of the shift as it happened. My solidity, my firm sense of self, melted away, made invisible by heat and pain and quiet perseverance. Vaporized. As we all are eventually.

Our brokenness leaves us as vapor, water crystals held high aloft, infinitesimally alone in our experiences, yet unknowingly drawn together. The knowledge of sorrow, of the high cost of love and life and freedom, wraps around, binds, bids us to lean in across generations and continents and military branches and airplane seats. Our daily, almost-civilian lives hum loud, quiet our stories. But beneath the droning of daily life, the need still beckons: to share a glimpse of knowing with those who, too, were remade by this existence. To connect over histories we keep safely folded and tucked away, awaiting a crack in the humming. As we gather our stories, we create something, form meaning from loss as we drift above a world unseeing.

The man in 19D—husband, father, grandfather, veteran, and Army colonel—and I sit, quietly pensive as we reflect on memories still unspoken, those still folded away on wrinkled sheaves, hidden deeply in pockets that may never see daylight. Yet we know. That our stories are part of the whole, that we ourselves are seen, if only for a glancing moment. That is enough. It must be.

We begin our descent, and as we pass through clouds, the plane shudders a bit, then steadies. The ground below is a patchwork of browns, small hills in the earth like crusty scabs, formed over wounds not quite healed. The mountain range stands in the distance, crowned with snow, silent.

I glance at faces as I exit the plane, all souls carrying unspeakable weight, this overflow of sorrow and joy together in one cup. We are children balancing too-full glasses filled to the brim. We pretend we can carry it all, while hoping nothing will jostle. And when the jostling happens, which it always does, and our cups tip, we wonder why we held them so closely, for what seemed too messy is really mead, a balm as hearts split wide.

This cup, mingling hideous truth mixed with all that is most dear, is our commonality. It bids us to gather, pulled together by invisible threads to offer remembrance as benediction. Crystal joins crystal in a magnificent link of sparkling lives. Together, these fragments form ever-shifting mosaics of purpose and struggle, beauty and loss, as we lift our memories high, high aloft, far above our fevered lives, to remind us again and again that yes, you too, and yes, even so, and a thousand more assurances. Assurances that we are not alone, and that nothing—no person, no moment—is ever truly lost.

Poetry

Poetry Winner

Bill Glose

What the Bomb Wants

The bomb never dreams of vacations
in Maui, of climbing ancient volcanoes
to peer into pools of lava. Why beauty exists
in one eruption and not another
could exasperate the bomb, but doesn't.
The bomb is busy counting seconds
till its annunciation to an unsuspecting crowd.

Spend time in the company of bombs,
you can't help thinking like one yourself.
Bag and tag ears and toes, amorphous chunks
and splintered bones. Guess which tab
fits which slot. Stagger-stumble-lurch
like a newborn calf uncertain how to walk.

As you shove shocked and curious
onlookers back from the perimeter,
your mind ticks toward detonation,
taking in the robes, the hands,
the dark-eyed faces, wondering
which is thankful for your presence,
which wants you dead.

Not all bombs have wires and batteries,
triggers connected to cell phone ringers.
Some attach to all you swallow
and hope to forget, biding time
in the roiling stew of your stomach.

Reason is secondary to a bomb. Resting
on a fulcrum, it waits for gravity to shift,
for the scale to totter and drop its weight,
for the chance to do the only thing it knows.

Poetry Honorable Mention

Aaron Wallace

The Blue Angels at Naval Air Station Jacksonville

October the twenty-seventh under a clear, clear, canopy
and my wife and I watch the F-18s twirl to hip-hop beats,
we smile like children do when they see a beagle puppy
stumble through grass, and I know that there is a young girl
who will never see a young dog—that girl I left on the rubble
pile of her school, that girl who wore black shoes
with a single brass button, that girl with the sequined hijab
stuck to the broken jigsaw puzzle of skull. She'll never sit
on her father's shoulders and point to the sky
with pretzel-salted fingers. At least she didn't suffer.
At least I stabbed her too-skinny thigh with the morphine
auto-injector, at least someone will remember her eyes,
and I hope she knows that I wanted to stay,
to peel off my gloves and hold the hands that could fit inside
my head, that I wanted to die on that twisted heap instead
of her, but I didn't. Instead I'm here, on the tarmac in Florida,
wiping pretzel salt off on my jeans while the performance
planes tear down the runway. The beer in my hand
is closer to water left in a plastic pouch for too long, but I am
breathing the exhaust-filled air and I am feeling my wife's skin
on my own. That girl is here too, but she isn't a broken body.
She is weaving among the crowd, playing peek-a-boo with the hem
of my wife's teal dress and laughing, her teeth intact now.
I try to laugh with her. I try to smile, and I reach for her hand.

Poetry Honorable Mention

Wes Smith

The Watch

We picked on Shawn because he shaved
his legs to swim laps in the Olympic
pool. "Less resistance," he'd say. After
the desert, exposed to chemicals
on wind in the smoke from burning rigs,
he was back in Germany. He'd lost so much
weight, his skin hung off him, hair falling out
in clumps—he couldn't climb a set of stairs.

At evening chow, we'd say, "The *fuck* is Shawn?"
and one of us would look in the latrine,
the dayroom, in his single, where we would
find him in his ratty cloth chair, clicking
a stopwatch he'd brought with him from Des Moines,
until the day we found him slumped,
the watch dropped on the floor, face shattered.

Lisa Stice

Measures

and means—quantifications
in the action phase: time between
arrival and what will come later

laid out chronologically and refined
to a standard—addressed then
redressed to fit the form already made

there then here in civil augmentation
in contracted support in combatant
logistics—dispatched to frays, edgings

Lisa Stice

Got Your Six

I burn my hand on the kettle
and you ask if I'm okay

yes, those sorts of wounds heal
to a shiny pink spot on my palm

sooner than we know it is gone
until someone reminds us

like when we met and I asked
the cause of the two long scars

on either side of your arm and
you told me of your rugby injury

how first you heard the crack
long before you felt the pain

but I barely notice those marks
now after these years except

when I fear you will hurt yourself
again especially when you're far

away and I'm not there to ask
if you're okay or see you shake it off.

J. F. Connolly
The Night We Fell in Love with Diana Ross

The dance floor was white, the Rexicana's
pine bleached and shuffleboard slick:
We slid across the Rex's floor
like Bandstand kids, jukebox dancers beneath
Dick Clark's smiling eye. In penny loafers
we clicked our heels to her "Baby, baby"
and sidled up to her throne on the stage
as if to say the world is changing.

We were taken by the Motown sound,
a rocking that we took and made our own.
We thought we were Jackie Wilson singing
"Lonely Teardrops." We were eighteen.
We knew nothing—it was years
we would learn how to get lost in a woman.
Whatever suffering was we could not
hear it in in her beating
beat of "Stop in the name of love."
Her voice called out "Come see about me"
and "Baby, baby, where did our love go"
held us in a night supreme—and kept us
in a blinding refrain, boys who would don
fatigues and carry M-16s, young men
who were still learning that the color
of love is the color of sound.

Jocelyn Corbin

Another Tour

A teary kiss farewell
My hands won't stop shaking
How'd I lose him again?
My heart won't stop aching
How do I explain this?
They've heard it all before
But do they comprehend
They've called him up for more?
Gazing beyond our fence
He sees a dad at play
He dreams of spending time
With his own hero someday
He hears someone sulking
Comforts little brother
We must not cry right now
We must be strong for mother
The news is soon forbidden
By the fear of seeing more
With three tours behind us
It's never easy to endure
The baby kicks inside me
A reminder left behind
We thought this would be over
Having hope made us blind
Mommy, I can't sleep again
He climbs up in my bed
Mommy, it will be alright
His hand upon my head
When will winter end this year
And why is it so cold?
When we will be whole again
I believe not what I'm told

Mary Ellen Talley
"We're just self-replicating carbon units"
*—The Canon, A Whirligig Tour of the Beautiful
Basics of Science* by Natalie Angier

Lucky for my sister
your son was at the house
to apply chest compressions and mouth to mouth.

They wheeled your body
into the emergency room
and finally stopped trying—

Medevac pilot who inhaled
Vietnam defoliants
and came home to Kathy Jo.

*The strongest bond in nature
the covalent bond, when two atoms team up*
(a marriage that lasted?)

Some kind of electromagnetic self-sufficiency,
soon sharing a pair or more electrons
(your three adult children?)

*As a rule, elements are more stable
and less reactive while in a bonded relationship.*
(I was your flower girl in 1957

and wouldn't talk to you for two years
because you stole my sister
from our fractured house.)

The 2nd Law of Thermodynamics
reassures us your molecules remain.
Your daughter's Facebook post of you

but not in present tense
brought me to a sudden grief
though you were ashes
by the time I arrived
in Texas for your funeral.

Mary Ellen Talley
U. S. Navy Haibun

Two children sleep in unzipped sleeping bags on grandparent's camp cots this longest evening of the year. Books strewn beside each sleeper and one nightlight still lit. Their father calls from South Korea when finally off the submarine to take a turn on the internet. Sailor hopes to do a family face-to-face. Problem is his son and daughter are asleep this midnight. Their father leaves each child a message to last until the next port safe harbor.

deep water
blowing bubbles
gray metal homecoming

Jason Arment

Reports May Vary

When people first hear about the Fog
of war, questions regarding how our vision
changes arise because how can we not see
if they're friendly or not? & what do you
mean you didn't much care either way?

One Devil Dog slated to go over was like this
so quick to judge what can happen between flash
& the thunder of rifles hammering away
at nothing & everything all at the same time
with the same tempo as running when our lives
depended on it, or chasing people down the street
when nothing depends on it, or us, or anything
but fighting for the sake of itself & losing

Because what other hill is there to die on
Because there aren't enough reasons to make me think twice
Maybe there is no because—I don't think
that far ahead to have anything but impulses
raw nerves twitching & an attitude problem

Jason Arment

More Than Enough

People ask me where I'd be if I hadn't joined
The Marine Corps when I was seventeen
& I always say I don't think about it
Not once, not even for just a second
No one believes me when I say this

It's as if they've separated the USMC
From what it does & how
Because if I were going to consider
Alternate realities the first place I'd go
Would be an uninterrupted night's sleep

Maybe I'd think of how it would be if
We hadn't left Iraq to the dogs & instead
Kept our word, installing a real democracy

Maybe I'd imagine the friends I lost
To that pointless war to have died
For something instead of for nothing

Maybe I'd bring Zube back, appear the instant
Before he pulled the trigger to beg him
To think about an apathetic future

But I sure as shit wouldn't daydream
About what pointless job I'd have in the middle-of-nowhere
Or if I'd be dead or in jail or married with children
Because there's no future where I didn't join the Corp as a kid
& if I wanted to think about things that don't exist
The power void known as Iraq is more than enough

Jay Harden

The Unknown Hero

My soul is the part
        that has free will,
        not me,
        and it says
        there is no blame,
        that blame is someone else's voice
        and not a fact,
        but a judgment for control of me.

A given love casts out fear and trembling
        so now I can see
        that people are good
        and my world is safe.

I want to be my own hero
        and not be known for heroism.

Beside the Tomb of the Unknown Soldier
        I wish for a monument
        to the Unknown Hero
        where I, and all who wore the uniform,
        can secretly honor the self inside
        for the truth of service we have done.

Jay Harden

The Wrong Way Round

What happened to me happened there:
>hair and heart turning gray too soon,
>wave after wave of sky floating past,
>droning on with iron,
>as innocent as ignorant,
>just like you below—
>senses soaking sound and scenery,
>both of us players in a conflict of belief
>so sure and uncertain.

Are you more like me, I wonder,
>or less than I imagine,
>as my mirror asks the same?

So, hailing bombs,
>I go to my Arc Light destiny
>just like you,
>me to live and you to die,
>or do I have it
>the wrong way round?

Bill Glose

Shark-Mouthed Skies

I grew up overseas
on Air Force Bases,
racing my bike
on runway's edge,

my father
streaking overhead
in an F4 Phantom,
a camouflage bullet

with a shark's mouth
painted on its nose.
All boys want to be
their father,

as if wanting alone
were enough
to lift them
into sky,

to score the blue
with white contrails
and leave proof
of their passage.

Bill Glose

Jungle Nights

The Army sent me to Panama,
where stitched-tight canopies
in steamy jungles
sewed out the sun,

where snakes serpentined fat limbs
and missile-nosed fish
torpedoed the roiling
torrents of streams.

As spider monkeys
howled overhead,
we carved damp earth
and climbed inside,

one man curled
in foxhole's bottom,
the other on guard
for vampire bats,

which longed to crawl
through crushed leaves
to suckle hot necks.
In night's womb,

amid the snicking
of a million millipedes
and a billion ants
carrying the world

in their jaws,
I finally understood
our transitory nature,
how tiny we all were.

Valerie Young

IGY6 (I GOT YOUR 6)

For those times we laced up our military boots
To digging and being in the foxhole all night our struggle symbolizes our truth
I GOT YOUR SIX

For the BLOOD, SWEAT, and TEARS we put into each deployment
To the stateside injuries: our fight to avoid sick call, we left OUR imprint
I GOT YOUR SIX

For those stressful situations: "if you got em smoke em"
To our long hikes and our cadence marches our rhythm is within
I GOT YOUR SIX

If it's not raining, we ain't training is a motto we live by
Working hard enduring so much pain we fight versus Questioning why
I GOT YOUR SIX

For the times we had to defend our life and kill
To those who LOST their lives but remain strong willed
I GOT YOUR SIX

From my mentality: 1st kill "I didn't kill a man but killed a target"
To the cold night sweats, those triggers were reminders making me not forget
I GOT YOUR SIX

22 symbolizes the mass suicide of our military vets
This sort of awareness need be displayed simply because our sacrifices inherited much debt
I GOT YOUR SIX

From fighting for our country to developing Post Traumatic Stress Disorder or PTSD
To making the ultimate sacrifice of not knowing IF we will live for the country's sake or be FREE
I GOT YOUR SIX

For those who made it back stateside experiencing adjustment issues
To the triggers of military dues we made, we may have long-term issues
I GOT YOUR SIX

My battles, my comrades:
I GOT YOUR SIX

Ryan Stovall

Bullet

Bullet,
    who slapped rock zipped up burrowed through my thigh,
and rocket,
    who blasted dirt desert rock coarse grit into my calf,
you came to be
    before I reached desert crossed wadi climbed mountain,
before I got to see my first child
    burning beside a VBIED-thrashed fuel bladder—

burning,
    but alive—
before my buddy
    died gasping hairy sweaty scared.

Before I could
    not save him.

Like me
    you were violent sons born in peaceful lands,
and like me
    they smuggled you in under the darkest night,
and like me
    they laid you down as potent fertile anti-seed,
to sprout
    and blossom a plentitude of future deaths.

A dozen dozen times—
    so many, too many!
I've interred
    as they intended.

And yet. . .
    I'm still here.

But you,
    where are you,
beside the bits
    residing in my leg?

My scars
    all scream you've failed.

Ryan Stovall

Two, or More

He's Hescoed in behind his lectern,
microphone, and horn-rimmed glasses,
this owl, mumbling inane gibberish,
spewing in place of poems
a broken sewer pipe's cold gush—
unintelligible slush, slanted cock-eyed diction
incapable of touching or cutting
to the bleeding quick one's intellect or soul.

I'd need at least two beers
to get into this, I whisper,
bare minimum. My Army
buddy nods, rolls his eyes.

Finally, it stops.
In closing, a second owl stands,
and praises his pure courage
(context—self examination),
admiring at length the nerve it takes
to write such poetry and
"unflinchingly contemplate
the craven void within us all."

I pick at an Afghanistan shard
stuck *just* underneath my skin
until I'm bleeding my disgust
at sheltered ivory tower fools.

Wes Smith

First Glimpse

We looked down into the valley
where command said the city
was located. We couldn't see
a city, we saw obliteration,
rubble with people scurrying
about, ant-like. From our
perspective, we couldn't tell
what they were doing, we just
knew they were there. Then
they stopped moving, looked
up at our position, and began
to scatter. Holmer scanned
the area with binoculars, *They're
gone, every single one of them
is gone. Don't they know we're
here to help?* He lowered
the glasses, shook his head. *I
don't think they do*, I said.

Elise Hempel

The Sign Painter

Trained to target beauty,
to measure and align,
on Okinawa my father
gripped a T-square surely
in his slender hand and aimed
a paint brush at a board,

and in Korea joined
men from every trade,
the ones he heard return
each night in silent piles
on the endless rumble of wheels,
those men with other skills.

Lindsey J. Medina

The Cost of War

My grandfather was
    too poor,
    too brown,
    too systemically uneducated
for anything but the Army.

He learned
    the ins and outs of English,
    the ins and outs of a rifle,
    the ins and outs of survival
at the same time.

When you fight for your life in
    Korea,
    Vietnam,
    America,
you start to figure out the one who is supposed to die is you.

You were
    never American enough anyway,
    rising through the ranks,
    a little less expendable,
the dirt stuck between America's teeth.

The end of a war on foreign soil
    only means a new one starts here,
    only means they'll die another way:
        a hole in the stomach forged by hunger
        a hole in the head. The
    only means to drain the blood—
        it may be yours.
        it may be someone else's.
        it may be God's.
None of this is God's. All of this is God's.

You can
    send a man to war,

  send him to steal food for his men, and give him a Medal of
    Honor when (if) he gets back.
  send him to jail for doing the same thing.

The only difference is what uniform he's wearing:
  Green or
  tan?
  Dollars or
  pennies?

They bleed red for
  the white men in blue suits signing
    the death sentences of men and women they can't legally kill on
      home soil,
  the men and women
    who just won't die of poverty
    who just won't die soon enough.

The difference between a foreign war and the one down the street is
  which one the government is willing to pay for,
  the difference is where the bodies are buried.

I got a sunburn last week on leave and was legally fined, cited as *damage to government assets.*

I am no longer human; spine contorted, a dollar sign in a uniform.
  There's a reason we wear camouflage.
  There's a reason that it's green.
  There's a reason war feels like sport when we're boxing a silhouette.

What if every war took a breath so deep
  its lungs burst into laughter,
  so full it woke its victims up from their sleep?

And what if
  we stopped fighting,
  we cleaned our rifles and never reloaded,
  the Sergeant is allowed to survive,
  we took back every gunshot,
  we gave a hug to every child whose family was torn from their
    tomorrows?

I ask my grandfather if it was worth it.

He tells me the bullet in his body only cost
    a bad knee,
    a lifetime,
    $0.21.

Lindsey J. Medina

Friendly Fire

It was a muggy morning the day we learned to low crawl. He had time, training, and a temper. A taut rope tightened over and under an old metal bed frame, where he taught us how to make a rack, how to tuck the excess under the foot end of the mattress, how to say *yes, sir*, when we wanted to say *no, sir*. We buried our bodies into the ground like the soldiers who already slept there. We, caked in camouflage and conflict, weren't in the backyard anymore, this was war. The mud-soaked morning we learned to low crawl, she dove under the rope, her throat wide open, howling staggered battle cries of the still beating hearts below. She swallowed sludge, and pride, and orders, but all I noticed was the dirt stuck between her teeth and how not everything had to be ugly in wartime.

Benjamín Naka-Hasebe Kingsley

Fall

Barberry bushes have been trampled all day
and some boys along the creek
pretending it is the barbed wire of an Indian prison
lie prone clutching nickel-plated revolvers
imaginary of course. Unlike our Reservations
about choosing the wrong side of this battlefield.
Cowboys gallop red across the stripped horses
of their pink legs embarrassing Indians
into a shirtless whoop of bows and
arrows falling dead BANG BANG
barbs fired from prepubescent lips.
Swimming in the music of a clear October
morning eagles handcuff the sun
bald as our understanding
of war never ending ever was.

Randy Brown

9 Things Uncle Sam Taught Me

Take quick showers.
Pack extra socks.
Drink water.

Mission first.
Safety first.
Family first.

The worst thing about getting wet
is getting wet.

It's better to ask forgiveness
than to ask permission.

The only True Threats are those against
life, limb, and eyesight. Everything else

is gravy.

Eric Chandler

Presentiment
Elegy for Lieutenant Colonel Charles L. Chandler, age 24, Battle of the North Anna River

"Not long before his death,
he talked with me about presentiments."

a thundershower hit while he fought
so I was glad it rained on me
when I visited the battlefield
for the first time

"He believed that no man would fall in battle
without having some impression beforehand of his fate."

as they forded the river
a belt floated by
containing a revolver
and a bayonet

"He said that his impression was
that he should live through the campaign, . . ."

he kept the pistol and
"jokingly" offered the bayonet
to some of his troops
just hours before the fight

". . .though he had a presentiment he should lose an arm."

his boss got drunk
and asked permission to attack
the division commander said no
the drunk ordered my relative to charge anyway

"I laughed at him;
but he seemed to think there was something in it."

I looked up the hill from the creek bed
steep as a flight of stairs

fifty yards to the impregnable trenches
drunken madness

"Had his arm shot off." —*New York Times*

I stood in the ravine
where his doomed charge fell apart
and repeated his words out loud:
I am going to rally my men and try to make a stand.

"Had his arm shot off below the elbow." —*Boston Journal*

I thought speaking his words
in the barren woods
under the overcast
would summon . . . something

"It also tore off Chandler's arm below the elbow." —Gordon C. Rhea

he died in enemy hands a few hours later
at Hanover Junction, a nearby train crossing
I also stood there in the dark rain
and looked at the wet steel rails

"His arm was broken, and hung motionless by his side; . . ."

his men tried to carry him as they were overrun
he said this to them but I heard it too
as I crouched and dipped my hand in the brook:
You can do nothing for me. Save yourselves if you can.

(Background and unattributed quotes are from a letter written by A. H. Dashiell Jr., Chaplain, 57th Massachusetts Volunteer Infantry on June 28, 1864.)

Jonathan Tennis

Birth of the Nuclear Age

Enola Gay Tibbets
gave birth to a man
who would one day
pilot a plane by her name.
He carried a Little Boy
across the Pacific
and laid him down to rest
on a city named Hiroshima.

Jonathan Tennis

First Reading

Between a comedian who wasn't funny
And a folk singer who was
I read my published poems
About war and a wife and a life
That by then seemed so far away.

Wrapping my fingers around the mic
I pled my case that night
That this too shall pass
Poetically.

Scott Ennis

Leadership

"The problem is the fucker didn't blow,"
says Sergeant Hansen, giving us his look
of "stupid private-dickheads." But we know
he's smart enough to fix it by-the-book.
The dynamite looks like a pile of shit,
although the turds are perfect tubes of red.
There's forty-seven stinking pounds of it
all heaped downrange. Which one of us is dead?
We "dickheads," who are certain that the blame
for all that unexploded shit should fall
on someone else, still wait to hear the name
of which of us will check the fuse. The call
comes quickly as our sergeant gives a shout:
"You dickheads wait right here. I'll check it out."

Sarah Colby

Two Wars Behind Glass

You are pixels forming and re-forming into yourself on the far side of the blue screen and not sitting across from me on the green chair full of prayers stockpiled in tumbled laundry. Years before there was Skype, it was your father in the distant glow and we had to wait a long turn in line for our ten minutes out of the year to see his face and if we were lucky maybe ten more in three months, fingers pressed to the cold glass of his cheek when we should all have been skipping smooth sandstone across the pond in the high desert hills up the road past the house, and the dog too, muddy and panting, pink tongue lolling sideways from a sloppy grin, the hot summer air all dusty juniper and evening primrose blooming yellow into the violet night.

Aaron Wallace

Grub Burger

is across the street from the Brain Clinic where they strap
the magnets to my head and make me tell the stories
of that year in the desert, over and over and over again
into the camera and boom mic above my head.
There is a blue cheese balsamic burger, medium-rare,
waiting for me, and the other patients, where we eat
burgers, shoestring fries, and the largest milkshakes
money can buy, enough to feel full of something other
than sand and visceral fat boiled in depleted uranium.

After the first week the servers knew us by name
and screamed at the kitchen to drop more patties
like running dry was going to get them killed.
We ignored the cruel comments about our appetite,
the whispers about hunger and the electrode adhesive
behind my right ear. There is more than glue stuck
beneath my skin, but the staff can't see the red wire
tucked into the back of a rocket, or the blood that runs
out of the burger and through my fingers.

Aaron Wallace
A Poem to the Tracer Rounds of Rayhana Park

When I miss the firefight,
remember the rendered fat of my

tempered past; a hundred tugs
of the tripwire for anyone with a temper—

If I miss the casualties of my convoy,
my people who sing through mouth-blood,

who plan with bloomed poppies, for
a burial of our spent shell casings—

If I miss the inhale of ultra-light Gitane Blondes,
remember the moment a shell strikes my

grid square of skin—You,
are the precentor of patriots,

the defender of my kin. You
are the fissures in the fierce

bones. Counting oleander petals by ones,
eyelashes by the dozen, and you ricochet

beside me, your red light reverberates
in the porcelain carousel of horses.

Photography

Photography Winner

Bree Pye

Sugar Rush

Kandahar, Afghanistan—December 19, 2010: A young Afghan girl enjoying her first piece of candy ever during a ribbon-cutting ceremony for a new medical clinic in Kandahar City.

Photography Honorable Mention

T. S. Johnson

Day Job

SSG Daniel Borthwick of 3-159 Attack Reconnaissance Battalion loads the AH-64D Apache Helicopter with 30mm cannon ammunition rounds during exercises in Kuwait, 2012.

Photography Honorable Mention

James Hugo Rifenbark

Documenting Work on the Saigon River

Army Specialist Stevenson, a motion picture (84 C) photographer, documents U.S. ships working on the Saigon River from a Mark II river patrol boat, June 1971.

Combat Lifesaver Training

A. Sean Taylor

A. Sean Taylor

Baghdad Lights

A. Sean Taylor

82nd in Iraq 2015

Rachael Attanasio
Echo 232 Tusker Medics' Graduation Ceremony

Those Who Served

Joseph S. Pete

Mourners

Joseph S. Pete

Joseph S. Pete

The War Correspondent

T. S. Johnson
Weekend Pass

Soldiers Thomas Johnson, Mykel Obert, and John Jenkins hike the Appalachian Trail with their military gear while out on weekend pass from Assigned Individual Training at Fort Eustis, Virginia, 2011.

T. S. Johnson
Finding Shade

Members of 10th Field Artillery seek shelter from the sun ahead of a live fire exercise with 3-159 Attack Reconnaissance Battalion, United States Army, in Kuwait, 2012.

Praying Soldier

Bree Pye

Kandahar, Afghanistan—August 30, 2010: An unknown chaplain's assistant praying over the coffin of one of our fallen warriors before his final dignified transfer home.

Unexpected Playmate

Bree Pye

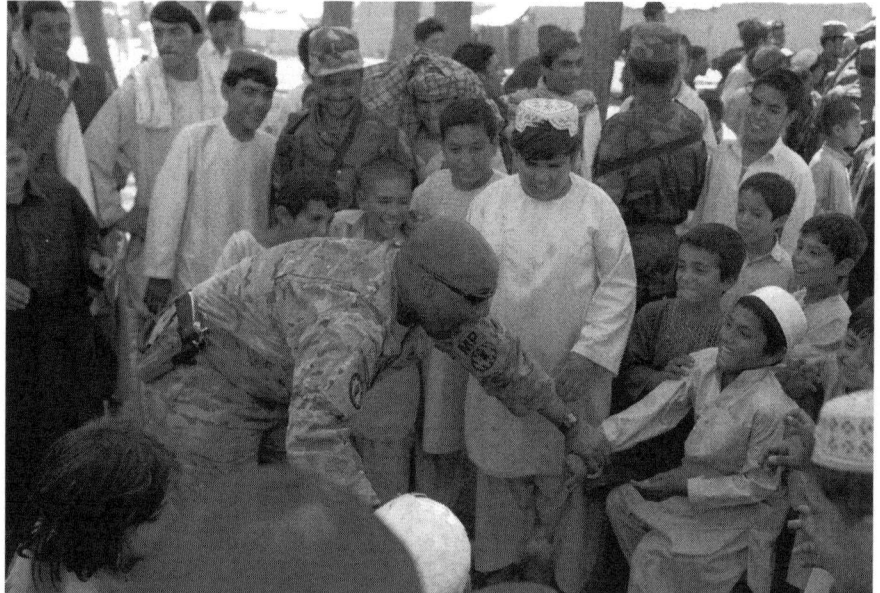

Kandahar, Afghanistan—June 8, 2011: Capt. Derrick W. Dew, Commander, 202nd Military Police Company, playing with young residents of the "Old Corps" area of Kandahar City during a ribbon-cutting ceremony for a new soccer field there. The new field was one of many projects headed by TF "Raider" and their Afghan National Security Forces partners in their joint reconstruction efforts to improve quality of life, safety, and security for residents of Kandahar City.

Interviews

Interviews Winner

Billie Holladay Skelley
Keith Eugene Fiscus: A Life of Service

Early Life:
I was born on October 6, 1925 in Fredonia, Kansas. My parents were farmers and we had a big family. There were nine children—six boys and three girls. I was the fourth oldest of the children. As a kid, I milked cows every morning and rode a horse several miles to school.

I was in high school when Pearl Harbor occurred. I wanted to join the Army right then and serve because I felt they needed me, but the superintendent of our school said I had to wait. He said I would be more useful after I graduated. He was able to get our class a deferment until we finished high school.

I graduated from Sedan High School in 1944. On the day of our graduation, we walked across the stage to get our diplomas, and then the able-bodied boys walked right out the door to an Army bus that was waiting for us.

I was ready. I wanted to go. I wanted to serve.

The bus took us to Coffeyville, and then we traveled to the Fort Leavenworth, Kansas, induction center. Once there, I took a standardized test, and they said I did well on it. They asked me if I'd like to try Intelligence and Reconnaissance Training School, and I said, "If I can serve the Army best that way, I will."

World War II:
I spent five weeks in training in Little Rock, Arkansas, at Camp Joseph T. Robinson, and by the fall of 1944, I was in France, attached to the Third Army. Most of the time I assisted the 94th division. The first thing I heard when I arrived was a gruff voice asking, "Where is that Fiscus boy who is going to be my intelligence officer?"

It was General George Patton, and I quickly learned to respect his ability as a commander. In my opinion, he was the best commander in World War II. I say that because he always was so involved in leading our company.

We were moving north and clearing out German units as we went. When Patton needed something, it always seemed like he would call on me. Sometimes I wondered why he didn't call on someone else!

During one of my first encounters with the enemy, General Patton informed me there was a German sniper in a nearby village who was firing at our soldiers. Patton wanted the sniper eliminated. I got to the area and figured if I could see the flashes when the sniper was firing his gun, I could try to stop him. I watched, saw the flashes, and took a shot with my rifle. The flashing stopped, and I thought, "I got him." I felt something hit my head, but I didn't know what it was, and it didn't register as important. I started walking back and a fellow soldier told me I was bleeding. He said I must have been hit, but I said, "No, the sniper missed me." This soldier said I should take a look at my helmet, and when I examined it, I found a huge hole. I also discovered I was bleeding. I may have got the sniper, but he got me, too. He had shot right at my head! I was lucky, however, because his bullet had curved when it hit the liner of my helmet. It just grazed me and came out near my ear. It nicked a blood vessel on the side of my head. When I informed General Patton about my helmet and head injury, he said, "Get another helmet, and let's get going."

Later that fall, General Patton told me that he needed intelligence about the enemy's current activities and movements. He said to me, "Bring me a prisoner." So I went behind enemy lines and found a prisoner. This prisoner turned out to be a young boy—around fifteen to seventeen years old—but he informed General Patton that the regular soldiers had moved north, taking their trucks and tanks for a strike in ten days. The young fellow told Patton they had snow tracks on. Patton called Eisenhower and told him the Germans had snow tracks on their tanks, and they were going up into snow country.

Eventually, I realized this "strike" was in Bastogne, Belgium. They ended up calling it the Battle of the Bulge. It was so very cold that December—freezing, snowy, and foggy, and so slow going. The tanks didn't work well in the cold, and they had trouble getting any traction. There were cries everywhere of "Keep your ground, stay alive, and don't retreat." Patton told everyone to watch their fuel and ammunition because the Germans didn't have any fuel or ammunition other than what they were carrying. He said if we could hold on and drag it out long enough, they'd be dead in the water. We kept hearing: "When the sun comes out, we'll get our fighters in the air. Just hold your positions till the fog lifts, and when the sun comes out, we'll end this war." They kept telling us there would be air support, but the fog was so thick for a time, we couldn't get any help from our air forces. They couldn't see us to drop supplies or anything. Finally, though, the sun came out, and the sky was filled with so many aircraft fighters, it looked like they'd block out the sun. After they arrived, it was soon over. The Germans ran out of fuel and ammunition, but they did plenty of damage before they ran out.

As officers were killed in the war, you moved up in rank with field promotions. As General Patton's personal intelligence officer, I soon found myself promoted to captain. General Patton even called me "his" captain.

Later, in the Saar Valley after Bastogne, I was ordered to take a concrete bunker. They called them pillboxes. This bunker had four-foot-thick walls, and there was a lot of artillery in it. We had tank destroyers that could blow the top off those bunkers, and then we would go in for any Germans that were left. I took a company, and I told my men to train their fire at the slits in the bunker, where the flashes of fire were coming out. I figured if we could keep their guns from firing for a bit, we could lay explosive charges and blow the door open. It worked and we succeeded in taking the bunker. It was snowy and cold outside, and I remember being so impressed when I entered that bunker with how warm it was inside those thick, concrete walls. Unfortunately, while I was in there, there was a German counterattack on the bunker. They put out so much artillery fire during their attack, I was knocked unconscious. When I regained consciousness, I realized I had been captured by the Germans.

My German captors knew I was in intelligence and reconnaissance, and they had one question for me: "Where are your divisions located?" They wanted to know the location of the American units, but I told them, "I can't tell you." They said, "We'll send you to a place where they'll make you talk."

I was moved to southern Germany, to Stalag 8 in the Dachau concentration camp, where I was forced to give up all my clothes and belongings. They took my dog tags and everything else I had. New arrivals had to hand over all their possessions. It was crowded there, and the living conditions were terrible. I was given a striped outfit to wear that reminded me of pajamas. Someone took my shoes, and I remained barefoot from then on. I was assigned a bed in a barracks where the beds consisted of wooden boards on a raised wooden frame.

Once they got you in Dachau, they made it clear there was no way out. There were many days when I wondered if I would survive. There were many nights when I thought I wouldn't.

Stalag 8 was filled mostly with Allied soldiers, but there were several nationalities held in the camp—Americans, British, Polish, and other groups. The Jewish prisoners were kept separate from the Allied soldiers. A Jewish preacher told me early on not to make any friends in the camp because they likely would not be there long. You never knew how it was going to end for anyone. They never told us anything. We had no idea what was going on in the camp, in the war, or in the world.

The German method for getting POWs to talk involved daily beatings and starvation. Their interrogations were brutal, and their methods were painful and terrifying. Many prisoners suffered terrible atrocities, and many died. I saw many men executed.

Every day, the routine was the same. They'd ask me the same question, over and over, about our troop movements and division locations. I would give only my name, rank, and serial number. When I didn't answer, they would beat me.

I got beaten daily—usually with the butt of a rifle, mostly about my face, head, and shoulders, and especially by my ears. Occasionally, they'd hit my knees with a gun butt. Every day, they would rough me up pretty bad. When I couldn't talk, they'd say, "Take him back, and we'll get him tomorrow."

They didn't feed us hardly anything. I ate garbage and anything else I could find. I remember eating potato peelings and the tops of carrots that the Germans threw out in the trash. I also ate grass. I figured if the young cows could eat it, I could, too. I just wanted to stay alive—even if it meant groveling through the garbage and eating like an animal. Some of my fellow prisoners would say to me, "Don't grovel like that, don't let them see you down"—but I didn't care. I ate anything I could find, because I wanted to live. I wanted to stay alive.

When I first arrived at Dachau in February of 1945, I heard people mention the "blood ditch." There was a sign in the yard that even said "Blood Ditch." When I asked what the "blood ditch" was, I was told that I soon would find out. This statement turned out to be true. My fellow prisoners and I were required every morning to leave the barracks and watch as the German soldiers lined up Jewish prisoners along this ditch that was a couple of feet deep. They forced us to watch as they tortured these men. It seemed like the German soldiers were having fun at the expense of the Jewish prisoners—like it was a game. They'd shoot one in the shoulder, another in the eye, and another in the knee, just to prolong their suffering. They'd shoot their ears off. Eventually, they'd kill them, but it was like a sport to them. When the prisoners could take it no longer, they fell in the ditch. After they finished torturing them, the ditch would be filled with blood—that's why they called it the "blood ditch." They had people empty the ditch afterwards, and they used an incinerator to burn the bodies to ashes. It was terrible. It was the saddest thing I ever saw—disgusting, terrifying, and awful.

I was most scared when we began to hear that the Americans were approaching the camp. The Germans had big tanks, Tiger Royals, and the Americans had tanks, and I was worried if they started firing, we'd all be killed in the battle. I figured it would be my last day on Earth, just when we were being rescued.

When the Americans arrived and blew the gate open, however, the German tanks were all gone. They had moved them out. We were in the yard and we saw the Americans coming. They blew the door open and we were free. It was wonderful. We were liberated on April 29, 1945.

I was happy, but very weak. They said I looked awful. When I entered Dachau, I weighed about 180 to 185 pounds. When the U.S. forces arrived, I weighed 93 pounds. I was on my last legs.

I told the soldiers who liberated us that I wanted some food, a steak or a pork chop. I wanted some meat, but they said they could give me only a small amount of a fortified protein drink every few hours. The medical staff said that was all I could have. I was on a liquid diet for several weeks before they would let me eat solid food.

They put me in an ambulance and took me to Nuremberg. After staying at the hospital there and receiving therapy, I was able to sit up for a time, so I could fly on a plane. I flew on a light plane to Bedford, England, to an English field hospital. They gave me more care, and then they put me on a train to Glasgow, Scotland. Eventually, we got on a C-54 cargo plane, which had been specially fitted with built-in bunks. Those beds were so nice compared to what I was used to. In the cargo plane, we made four stops—Iceland, Greenland, Nova Scotia, and finally Fort Dix, New Jersey.

Once I was stateside, they gave me two choices for hospitals: O'Reilly General Hospital in Springfield, Missouri, or Winter Hospital in Topeka, Kansas. I don't know why, but I went with O'Reilly Hospital in Springfield. My family members were upset because they were still living near Fredonia, and Topeka would have been much closer to them. Most of my hospital recuperation, though, was at O'Reilly.

While I was there recovering, I was allowed to attend some classes at Southwest Missouri State Teacher's College. They said if we wanted to, we could sit in, as long as we didn't cause any disruption to the regular classes. I wanted to go to school, and I attended agricultural courses. I really enjoyed it. I figured when I got back home that I would farm like my parents, but I eventually realized that I was too beat up to farm. Physically, I couldn't do it anymore.

I still have pain in my shoulders from the beatings I received. One of my arms has a very limited range of motion. It hasn't been fully functional since the war. I can't swing it like normal. It just hangs. I also have pain in my knees from being hit there. One knee bothered me for decades. My lower jaw is shorter than my upper jaw, due to the beatings I experienced on my face. It is hard for me to get teeth that fit properly. My hearing also was damaged by the blows they struck around my ears with their gun butts.

I left military service in October of 1945. I was awarded two Purple Hearts—one for injuries sustained as a result of hostile enemy action and one for injuries sustained during my time in captivity.

After the War:

Once I finally regained my health, I remembered how much I'd liked those first classes, and now I had the GI bill, so I decided to go back to school. I returned to Springfield, Missouri, as a freshman at Southwest Missouri State College.

In one of my first introductory science courses, there was this girl who sat behind me. She was the sweetest, prettiest girl I ever saw. Her eyes sparkled, and her smile could melt an iceberg. She was out of this world. Her name was Pauline, and I eventually asked her to a Sweetheart Dance. We met at the dance on February 14, 1947, and we were married on June 23, 1947. Pauline was a nurse, and we were married for 65 years until she passed away. She's gone, and all of my brothers and sisters are also deceased. Sometimes, I wonder why I'm still here.

Anyway, they eventually said I needed to go back to Kansas to keep them from having to pay out-of-state tuition. So Pauline and I came back to Kansas, and I attended Kansas State University in Manhattan where I earned my Bachelor of Science and Master's degrees. I became an agriculture teacher in Kansas and taught high school for several years, but then I had an opportunity to attend the University of Illinois to obtain my PhD, so I went to Illinois.

I earned a doctoral degree in 1965 from the University of Illinois in horticulture and horticultural education, and then I spent years teaching at the college level. I taught at universities in Illinois, in Washington, and in Tennessee. I also taught in Africa. In Sierra Leone, I taught agriculture and set up agricultural education programs for four years. I also had a postdoctoral fellowship, from Illinois State, where I set up research activities and had advanced classes.

I enjoyed teaching and the opportunities it provided to serve. I think teachers perform a great service by helping people to improve their lives.

Later Life:

When I finally retired from teaching and returned to Kansas, I noticed they were building a big store in Coffeyville. It turned out to be a Walmart, and Sam Walton hired me to work in the garden center. It was a great opportunity, and I worked there for a year and a half. At that time, however, Coffeyville didn't have regular doctors in residence. Doctors came in only once a week to see patients, and Pauline wanted to live where there was a hospital and more full-time physicians.

So in 1992, we moved to Joplin, Missouri, and I have lived in Joplin ever since. I took a job in Joplin at Walmart Store No. 59, working in the garden center and as a store greeter. I've continued to work there right up to the present day.

I've worked for Walmart for over twenty-five years, and as long as I can be of service, as long as I can help people, I'm going to do it.

That's my story, such as it is.

After reliving all these memories, I'll have cold sweats, flashbacks, and nightmares tonight. I'll find it hard to sleep for the next few nights. I should be able to tell myself to stop, but it doesn't work like that. Memories of the war and the concentration camp still haunt me. They stay with me—even after all these years.

I think it is important, though, to share my story. It's important to tell about the war and to remember what happened. People forget, but they need to remember.

Sometimes I wonder why I survived when so many other soldiers died. I wonder why I'm still here when Pauline and all my brothers and sisters are gone, but then I tell myself, I'm still here because I have a story to tell, and it's a story people need to hear.

Some time ago, someone saw my POW license plates, and they thought the POW referred to a Native American tribal powwow. They didn't know what the POW stood for and that upset me. I knew then I had to keep telling my story no matter how many sleepless nights I had or how many nightmares I experienced.

Today, it is more important than ever to tell about what happened in the war, because soon, all the World War II veterans will be gone. There won't be anyone left to tell what really happened.

So, I have to speak now, while I can, because people need to remember.

Fiction

Fiction Winner

Robert Morgan Fisher

Artificial Reef

Truth is there'd been a time when Barney would've rejected Brink's offer outright. *Put that money toward something secure. Get some stability, for chrissake.* But now, Barney takes what he can get. There's not much time, he knows this. The daughter is fine as daughters go—producing three cherished grandkids and reliably consistent interaction. Even her husband is surprisingly solid.

But Brink? No, his son took a different path.

Barney told Brink, several years ago: I feel like I don't know you.

Scuba diving. Geez.

And Barney has only himself to blame. They were watching *The Undersea World of Jacques Cousteau* when Brink was fourteen. That led to the challenge from Brink, a father-son activity to pursue between deployments. They were both certified in record time. They both seemed to lose interest after that cruise, the one where Barney came back and could barely recognize his son. It wasn't just stature, heft and unshorn hair, it was the look in Brink's eyes. *Where is Brink?* thought Barney. *I want him back.* That was a rough patch, one of many.

So Barney and Brink haven't gone diving in fifteen years. At first, Barney thinks they're going to meet up in California, where Brink lives. But Brink has something else in mind.

Pensacola, Dad.

Pensacola? Why the hell there?

Think, Dad.

Barney went to Officer Candidate School in Pensacola, but Brink was a newborn at the time. He couldn't possibly remember anything about Pensacola.

Dad?

Thinking.

I'll give you a hint: Centurion.

Barney's mouth hangs open.

No.

Yes.

When Brink says that word, Centurion, an entire life segment unfolds like a map in Barney's mind: one hundred arrested landings on an aircraft carrier. That's what makes you a Centurion. Barney achieved that, and more, on a couple of ships—but no matter. Brink is referring to a specific carrier now resting at the bottom of the ocean, twenty-three miles off the coast of Pensacola. The first carrier where Barney made Centurion—Triple Centurion, by the time of his last cruise.

The Mighty O, says Barney.
Affirmative.
Super.
Can you handle it?
Hell yeah, I can handle it. Question is: can you handle it?
Oh yeah, old man, I can definitely handle it.
When?
Next month. Weekend of the 10th.
Weekend of the 10th ... weekend of the 10th ... Barney runs a Sharpie through those dates on the calendar, scrawls *Brink* over the line.

Now Barney drinks tiny bottles of vodka during the flight. He's well-prepared for this mission. The USS Oriskany is now The Oriskany Reef: a Fish Attractor facing due south. Most decommissioned ships get turned into Korean tractors, so this seems like an improvement to Barney. It is decided, somewhere over east Texas, he will push himself on this dive. The warnings about going no further than the flight deck do not apply to him, he reasons, because this ship was once his domain. Barney's certain he can do the dive blindfolded. He smiles, resting his eyes.

In Pensacola, after an hour of bloody marys in the airport bar, he sets out to meet Brink's incoming flight, he gets lost at first, finally locates the correct concourse. Brink saunters up from behind and says, Boo. Barney turns, relieved to see him. The hug is firm, full of pent-up playfulness. Barney steps back and says: Let me look at ya. He evaluates Brink's off-kilter grin, guitar case and duffel. Brink's clothes have the natty scent of fresh success. They repeat *How are ya's?* back and forth out of nervous excitement. Then Brink grabs Barney's gear bag and says: Wuh-ho, what's this?

Before Barney can stop him, Brink's unzipped it and pulled out a mask, flippers, snorkel. Barney reaches out.

Gimme that, you asshole.
No lemme see ... Dad, this mask—the seal's completely gone!
Brink starts chucking stuff into the trash, right there in the airport.
Hey!
Barney snatches at the bag.
There was nothing wrong with those flippers.
Dad.

I'm serious.
We'll be renting everything. Come on, let's get some chow.

It's the Waffle House. Brink talks Barney out of ordering oatmeal.
Man, I hate Florida, says Brink. Most worthless state in the union.
Why's that?
Hot, humid. It's sinking. It's a sand-spit, not a state.
Barney doesn't argue, he hates Florida too.
They don't talk about the 12-string—the Martin. When he was a junior in high school, Brink informed Barney that the ornate Japanese acoustics he'd brought back from overseas were just laminated plywood. And so, ignoring his wounded pride, Barney did his homework and arranged to have a Martin 12-string under the Christmas tree. It was a thing to behold. Barney and Brink had a few good years together with that guitar. Barney couldn't wait for the kid to come home with that Martin and play all the good songs. Then Brink went out into the real world; the Martin 12-string became a casualty of poverty. He sold it to make rent.
Over waffles, Brink asks: How did re-certification go?
Fine, just gotta take it easy down there.
How's the waffle, Dad?
Sucks.

That night, they stay at the Whiting Field BOQ. Brink insists on paying since the trip is his gift to Barney. The accommodations are acceptable, food's not bad. They stay up late in their room, drinking beer. Brink pulls out the guitar. Barney knows he should ask to hear Brink's hit song, but just can't bring himself to ask for it. In fact, as Brink's endless performance wears on, he grows more and more restless. He shouldn't feel this way, but he does. There's just something about Brink still hungering for his approval that makes Barney sick to his stomach. It's not fair, he knows that, and maybe it's the guitar itself: a new Martin D-35 six-string. Certainly not a 12-string—there'll never be another one like that 12-string—but the fact that this new guitar is a Martin stirs up trouble. Brink must have made a lot of money to afford such a guitar. He told Barney he'd quit his day job at the record store, traded the Intrepid for a Lexus.
How come you didn't get a 12-string?
Too hard to keep in tune, for one thing, says Brink.
I know.
They don't travel well.
Brink stops tuning, drains his beer. He puts the guitar away.

Hey, what are ya doin'? You're not gonna quit now, are ya? Barney's protest rings hollow.

We gotta get up early.

You sure?

Yeah. Let's hit it.

Later, as Brink sleeps in the next bed, Barney just can't get comfortable. When Barney does finally fall asleep, he dreams he's on a deserted, rocky beach at sunrise, forced to wait and watch as Brink swims out to sea.

It's only during the 7 a.m. gear-up at Scuba Shack that Brink begins to realize the full scope of his father's diving ambitions. Dives to the submerged Mighty O are generally limited to the flight deck and tower, but Barney wants the special nitrox mix.

You sure, old man? says the manager, called over after the clerk Brink and Barney have been dealing with throws up his hands.

Who you calling old man? Barney grins. We're both open-water certified and I personally got recertified for up to 200 feet, both professionally and— Barney produces the actual doctor's note—physically.

Well, well, well, says the manager, a Barnacle Bill type with soggy tattoos. My apologies, Commander. He turns to the skeptical clerk: Suit 'em up.

But before they leave, Barnacle Bill pulls Barney aside and says: Be careful down there, it affects different divers in different ways. You know that.

Roger.

On the way out to the chartered catamaran, Brink whistles low. 200 feet, huh? Sure you can handle it?

Hell yeah. Can *you* handle it?

Oh yeah.

Brink laughs and tries to help Barney hoist the tanks. They'll tie the extra tank to the anchor line, just in case.

How you feel? says Brink.

Great. Yourself?

Little hungover. You?

Not me.

Coolers of food and drink are loaded in by the first mate. Ropes untied from cleats.

Looks like we got some good weather, says the captain, as they shove off. Barney surveys the marina, sees several other dive shops, including one called Wet Dream.

So much for your conservative south, he says and nudges Brink.

That reminds me, says Brink. You know that movie *What Dreams May Come*?

I musta missed that.

With Robin Williams, remember?

Nope.

Last movie Barney saw was *Top Gun* and it was awful.

What Dreams May Come. All-time worst title for a movie. Anyway, part of the story takes place in Hell. Guess where the Hell scenes were filmed?

No telling.

On the decommissioned Oriskany.

No shit.

There are only two other people making the dive: a retired Chief Petty Officer who served on the Oriskany five years before Barney and a blonde woman. She has a crewcut, body-piercings, drove up in a purple Subaru. Barney zeroes in on the Chief, a black man, and they swap stories for everyone's entertainment.

I was there for the fire in '66, Chief volunteers.

Bet that was fun, says Barney.

Forty-four died.

Every ship has its fire, says Barney. Oriskany, Forrestal, Constellation…

I was evac'd to the Connie, says the Chief, displaying white scars on his arms.

He means evacuated to the USS Constellation, says Barney for the woman's benefit. He adds: I catapulted an A4 into the drink in '69.

Flameout? says the Chief.

Yeah, he turns to Brink. I ever tell you about that?

What do you think? says Brink.

Gulf of Tonkin, Summer of '69. Sank straight to the bottom, he addresses the woman again, she's interested.

The way you get out of the aircraft in that particular situation is to eject underwater. But just as I was about to, I look up and there's thirty-five thousand tons of carrier passing overhead. The props are unbelievably huge—and loud. Cockpit started to fill—punched out in the nick of time. I'll never forget it.

You okay? says the Chief.

Still have back pain.

The reflection of Barney's face fills the woman's mirrored sunglasses. Her mouth hangs slightly open.

Wow, she says.

Yeah, says Barney. That's what I said.

We don't need to dive, she indicates Barney and the Chief. The story's right here.

Oh, we need to dive all right, says the Chief.

The captain turns the helm of the catamaran over to the first mate and makes his way back.

Captain Fought delivers a canned speech about the history of the ship; how it was environmentally prepared to serve as a reef with all contaminants removed, including oil, aviation fuel, hydraulic fluids, mercury and PCBs.

Flight deck is one hundred-forty feet down, he says, below that you got your 01 and 02 decks and hangar at about two hundred feet. The interior is extremely hazardous and should not be entered under any circumstances. It is vast and intricate. Stick to the superstructure.

Is the interior even accessible? asks Brink.

In order to sink properly, no part of the ship could be sealed. So yes, it's accessible, but like I said, this is *not* a penetration dive.

He studies the extra tank sitting by Barney and Brink, glances at their flashlights.

You're all adults and open water certified. I can't tell you what to do. But we've never had a fatality yet on the Mighty O and I don't intend to be the first. Do I make myself clear?

As a bell, says Barney.

The sun is bright, but cannot fully illuminate the immensity of the Oriskany.

The scuttling has brought out the baroque aspects of the ship. Brink and Barney pass over mammoth faded deck letters: CVA-34. A fair-sized cobia comes straight at them. He looks to Brink and gives the *Okay* sign. Brink nods as he attaches the extra tank to the anchor line. Splash noises from above, as the two others enter the water. Barney descends as quickly as he can, as if trying to outrun a foe. Brink signals Barney to slow down, pointing to his wrist gauge, which is connected to a computer on his tank. Barney nods, checks his own wrist gauge, returns another *Okay*. Behind the mask, Brink sees something in Barney's eyes that he's never seen: boyish excitement.

At the flight deck, Barney achieves buoyancy above the catapult, gestures to Brink, attempting to communicate. Brink nods. Croakers, amberjack, triggerfish and mackerel swarm around Brink. They stand against the steady wind of ocean current, swirling a blizzard of plankton and mysterious white debris. Barney checks the wrist gauge, draws his flashlight and disappears over the edge of the flight deck, waving for Brink to follow. Brink hesitates, but only for a second.

Because it's still morning, port is better lit than starboard. More croakers, snapper, jellyfish ... They descend past bomb jettisoning ramps, winches, cargo booms; past the 02 Deck all the way down to the 01. Barney switches on his flashlight, looks back at Brink, who does the same. Barney shines the beam into a dark opening and spooks a grouper.

In they go.

Brink wishes they had radio transmitter masks so they could talk. Instead it's all gestures, dive signals, guessing... blanks presumably filled in later over lunch. Brink can see why exploration of the interior is discouraged: it's small, dark and difficult to maneuver with tanks on your back. In about fifteen minutes they'll have to turn around.

Barney thinks he knows exactly where his old stateroom is. He recognizes the way, even after the decay of decommissioning. Getting there is slow going, however, that's why he wasted no time getting down.

Barney wants to take in every rivet, every rusted iron railing and stairway, every soon-to-be-undone weld—but there's no time. You can almost hear the salt water doing its corrosive work. His heart thrills at every pulse of recognition: squadron ready room; linen locker; wardroom lounge; mess room. *I was here.* He recalls how the passageway was dimly lit, to preserve pilots' night vision. His flashlight illuminates familiar architecture and the cluster of staterooms. Hatchways and doors narrow—it's a tight squeeze every few yards, but not impossible. He looks back, sees Brink about eight feet behind. He presses on.

Suddenly, the biggest barracuda Barney's ever seen comes down the passageway, straight for his flashlight beam. Six feet long, at least; a hypnotic torpedo. Jagged underbite, teeth like shards of shattered china actually brush Barney's hand. He remembers a lieutenant jg in some tropical port, years ago, dangling barefoot off a quay. Felt something like a paper cut, pulled out a bloody stump, foot cleanly severed.

The barracuda glides past, then darts over to Brink's light. Instead of moving on, barracuda shadows Brink steadily. Barney signals *Okay?* Sends telepathic messages to Brink, hoping he'll remember that barracuda often do this with divers. Jacques Cousteau purrs inside Barney's head: *Their hope eez zat zee diver eez a fellow predator who will generate scraps of food.* Barney waits up for Brink, makes a reassuring gesture with both hands. Brink gives an uncommitted *Okay*, puts on the brave face. Barney's heart pumps. What talent! What a waste his boy's life has been. *You play guitar better than anyone I know...* Chasing the famous and the few... And the constant acrimony with his mother...

Why did it turn out this way? It's beyond him... There is interior pressure, a swelling of his soul. It seems like relief, an answer perhaps, is close by, hidden within, as if further on more will be revealed.

They push forward, Barney now less certain he knows the precise location of his old stateroom. Things are looking not-so-familiar. The urge to nap is suddenly very strong.

Now they are deep inside the 01 Deck of the Mighty O. Barney sweeps his flashlight beam along cramped walls and twin bunk beds. Nothing to prove it's his or anyone's particular stateroom and it's a letdown. A crab scuttles, barnacles and coral already colonizing. *The Bridges at Toko Ri*—that was the other movie they filmed on this carrier... *Fuck Hollywood... the story's right here. And it's over...* Barney floats over to the lower bunk. Brink, in the doorway, shakes his head, barracuda still over his shoulder. Barney's vision melts around the edges. He waves a grumpy hand. *Put light away...* Cousteau again with four words:

Rapture of zee deep...

Lips, tongue and mouth tingle into a nebulous numbness that extends to his fingertips. It occurs to Barney that he could own this stateroom, it's public domain now, like the moon. Nobody can make him leave... but why would he want to stay? Barney looks up, bottom of the upper bunk becomes the Oriskany that time he flamed out and sank to the bottom. He's back there now, sinking... spinning... shadow of the hull blocking out every last ray of sunlight like a sliding sarcophagus lid... *eject...*

By some miracle, Brink does not get lost in the labyrinth of passageways, and emerges with Barney out the starboard side. The barracuda is long gone.

Ascend, equalize... The gauge on Brink's wrist flashes with alarm. Brink discards Barney's weight belt, it sinks, caroms in slow motion off a tower bulwark, coming to rest on the ancient flight deck. Ahead, spare tank dangles on the anchor line, just out of reach. Brink's supply abruptly ends a good twenty feet out, optical receptors popping black and white.

They hang suspended. The edges of Barney's vision blur. A formation of fish becomes a dogfight. Below, the Mighty O molders, Queen of the Essex Class Carriers. The last clear vision Barney enjoys is of a nine-foot tiger shark, drifting by with an indifferent wag of its caudal. Barney's short-circuited mind morphs the shark into a dreadnought Martin 12-string. What did that salesman call it again? Oh yeah—*The most dangerous guitar ever made.*

Fiction Honorable Mention

Amie Charney

How to Schedule a Nervous Breakdown

Deployments are like pregnancy. The months leading up to d-day nearly run a similar course: wild mood swings, morning sickness, heartburn, everything swells, manic happiness, deep fears of inadequacy, sleepless nights, nesting, a gnawing desperation to fit everything in (before life changes for good), solicited advice and semi-solicited advice and unsolicited advice, endless fights, sleepless nights (yes, this must be said twice), and panic . . . heart-clenching, gut-wrenching panic.

Like most temperamental babies, deployment "spool-up" cooks until ready . . . no matter your mental state or preferred timeline. The delivery date is in flux, his seabag gets packed and unpacked and repacked twice again. The babysitter scheduled for your last romantic encounter rescheduled twice again. Well-meaning rounds of friend farewells rounded twice again. You beg the spool to stop, beg him just to leave, frantically beg the powers to induce labor—just get it started, just make the unknowingness stop.

It feels like progress when you start cataloging "the lasts." Those things that divide pre from post: that last visit to your in-laws, the last walk on the beach, the last Sunday communion, the last time he takes the garbage out. He makes 271 paper rings with the kids, one to tear off each day, and a daddy wall with all their favorite pictures together. Smiling epitaphs you'll have to hide if things go—you glue another 30 paper rings because 271 is optimistic. You make him the last supper, have a final toss or two or three (depending on how long you've been married), the last selfie, the last brush of skin, last kiss, last breath that mingles with his. The sound of his voice saying his last word—"you," and the sound of your voice saying your last word—"safe." Then that last look, bittersweet and longing, clenches at your throat. Those "lasts" will eat at you for another nine months because, although you'll probably have Pad Thai or buy shaving cream or pick out a new couch together again, you are acutely aware that everything will be different when you do. You will change. He will change. Us will change. "Our" will never fit like it did five minutes ago.

You memorize a new crease in his face, and remember a moment, right before your daughter was born. You were panting and pushing and perspiring, he was cringing at your pain . . . he kissed your hand, caressed his lips over your knuckle, and whispered, "It's almost over, honey," and you nearly screamed back, "It's only just begun." It feels much the same in this moment. You hold tightly to the optimistic platitude he uttered over d-day morning coffee, "Tomorrow will be one day closer to home with you"—but he is disappearing into adventure, and you are disappearing into endless laundry.

A lifetime is lived between his last look and long walk away. Especially since this one . . . this deployment . . . will be the longest he's ever been gone. Your brain loops the things he will miss: son's middle school graduation, end of school parties, his brother's ordination, summer vacation, daughter's birthday, his birthday, the first day of high school, driver's ed classes followed by the driver's license test followed by her crashing his car, burnt Thanksgiving turkey, boozy Anniversary, and all the Hallmark holidays that he scoffs at but you love. When he leaves, your daughter will be 15 and son 12. When he returns your daughter will be 16 and son 13. Or 10 and 7. Or 7 and 4. Or 18 and 15. And those are just the big events. He has missed, will miss . . . field trips, loose teeth, new teeth, skinned knees, two-wheel bike victories, braces on and braces off, her first freeway drive, her first date and first heartbreak, and prom.

The resignation in his shoulders as he turns away tells you he won't glance back again. And then, Poof! he's gone. A chasm of aloneness cleaves your chest open with the realization that those last moments could truly be "THE LAST." After seven deployment "babies" in eighteen-years of marriage—six of those seven being combat tours—you should have this down. What's combat tour number seven to you? Like all "good" career Corps wives, you don't even count the months of workups or training programs or selection boards or exercises . . . you eat those pesky detachments for lunch. Nor do you count the 2 a.m. phone calls or 5 a.m. humps or 10 p.m. night flights or arty fires that claim his time even when he is "home." You only count the long ones, your own battle scars. You'd think it gets easier but realize it just gets different.

The cord tightens around your neck, stealing breath until there is a tug at your dress . . . and you realize this unhinged harpy can *not* be you. You can *not* lose it. You are a Marine Corps wife, Semper Fi Do or Die, take the hill, marshal the troops. You are judged as a "good" or "bad" wife by how easy you make "the waiting" look. That little hand and cherubic face, splotched red with tears, reminds you that so much depends on your sanity. You have a DEFCON 2 plan ready—your sacred rules of engagement, firm. The first rule—no one dies on your watch, physically, spiritually, mentally . . . if no one dies, than everything else is gravy. Rule number two—pick the hill you want to die on. Whenever the laundry piles rise to K-2 heights, or you're scraping pre-Cambrian layers of Fruit Loops off your kitchen sink—ask yourself, "Is this truly the hill you want to make your stand on?" If you can live with it, then let it go until d-day #135.

Day 135, or hump day, is when you've scheduled your nervous breakdown. It's been planned for months. Your babysitter is booked. Your wine selection carefully curated, with an eye to chocolate pairings. Your husband's college sweatshirt and your fuzzy socks and old maternity sweatpants are waiting on your top closet shelf. Your girlfriends, carefully selected for their wisdom and snark, have prepared a chick-flick marathon meant to transport you through the five stages of grief. You can make it to Day 135. You readjust your Jackie O sunglasses, plaster a smile on your face, and, in a pseudo-sweet Southern drawl, ask the assembly of stoic women around you, "Who's up for some retail therapy?"

Fiction Honorable Mention

William J. Watkins Jr.

Sacrifice and Service (1941)

He arrived in Hampton Falls about three weeks after Pearl Harbor; it was a day or two after Christmas but before the New Year. He looked impeccable in the wool uniform. The jacket's chocolate-colored olive drab perfectly matched his eyes. The three chevrons on each shoulder signified a sergeant—a leader of men. The Windsor knot of the cream-colored mohair necktie was perfectly centered between the front spread of his collar. His every stride was one of brisk authority.

As soon as he stepped off the train, most everyone could guess his purpose. Considering the recent events, who could not understand? The News had already elucidated on the matter: death, malice, and cruelty had enveloped Europe and parts of the Orient. The president had done his best to stay out of the fray, the correspondents explained, but the Japanese had brought the fight directly to U.S. soil. America's peacetime army, barely large enough to defend the borders, needed augmentation. Even if every one of those soldiers already in uniform were a carbon copy of the heroes from the Great War, they still could not carry the full load. What the country needed, the people were told, was for young men to step forward and serve, and for citizens of all ages to sacrifice.

The Sergeant was something of a celebrity before he ever left the Hampton Falls station. A crowd of children immediately surrounded him on the platform. The boys did their best to stand at attention and salute. Offering a warm smile to his young platoon, the Sergeant crisply brought his hand to his hat with his forearm inclined at a perfect forty-five-degree angle. In the same smart manner, he returned his hand to his side.

Spencer Dye was at the station to see off his cousin Millie Dubois. As soon as he had said goodbye, Spencer joined the children in their adoration of the man in uniform. Of course, Spencer and the young ones were not the only folks with eyes on the soldier. Cousin Millie and several other ladies peered from the windows of the Pullman railcars with little or no attempt to disguise their thoughts about the dashing figure.

In his usual direct manner, Spencer strolled up to Hampton Falls' newest guest and introduced himself. "Soldier, I'm Spencer Dye. I just wanted to tell you what an honor and a privilege it is to have you in our town."

The Sergeant shook Spencer's hand. "I'm much obliged, sir. My name is Brandon Burns. You are very blessed to call this place home. As the train rolled through those mountains, I couldn't help but to be captivated by the scenery. I've seen a lot of this country since I've been in the Army, and your corner of it here is magnificent."

"I appreciate you saying that. If I do say so myself, there ain't no place like the Chauga Valley. You oughta see it in the fall when the leaves turn. There'll be colors and shades that you ain't never seen before."

"I'm sure it is beautiful. I'd love to see that one day." Sergeant Burns paused and adjusted his service cap so that it sat squarely on his head. The coat of arms affixed in the center glistened in the sun. "My mission," he continued, "is short term."

"Well, if I can help you in any way, just let me know. Are you waitin' on somebody to meetcha here?"

"Actually no. As I am sure you understand, the craven attack on December 7 has changed our national landscape. The War Department, with little time for logistical planning, has sent me and hundreds of others forth to directly address the citizenry and to prepare our people for the struggles to come. Unfortunately, no prior arrangements could be made."

"So, you ain't even got a place to stay?"

"Not at this point. If you could direct me to a boarding house or hotel, I'd be much obliged."

"Mrs. McCutchen has a room or two to let and that is a tolerable place." Spencer paused a moment and contemplated the situation. His eyes darted from the Sergeant to the boarding house just down the street.

"But the Missus and I would be honored to host you. My Cousin Millie just left us after her Christmas visit, so our guestroom is empty. No sense in the War Department spending money on a room when we're in a position to open our home to you."

"Mister Dye, on behalf of the United States, I thank you for this act of hospitality. I gratefully accept."

Spencer reached down and hoisted Sergeant Burns' duffle bag onto his shoulder and led the solider to Spencer's black Ford pickup truck. On the passenger door of the truck, Sergeant Burns noticed the white lettering: "Dye's Hardware."

"Mister Dye, your business wouldn't happen to be here in town would it?"

"It sure is. In fact, you can see my building just across the way next to Burchfield's grocery store. My daddy was a blacksmith in this town, but with more folks using manufactured equipment around these parts, the smithin' has become a smaller part of the business. So, about five years ago, I changed the name from 'Dye's Blacksmith Shop' to 'Dye's Hardware.' A man's got to keep up with the times or be passed on by."

"Could I impose on you to drive us down the Main Street area? I need to scout for a suitable location that the government could rent on a short-term basis for recruiting and war bond sales."

"How bigga space you need?"

"Not that much. All the War Department requires is that the space have a desk and a lock on the door for security purposes. Otherwise, I have discretion in selecting the site."

A toothy grin appeared on Spencer's face. "Well, it ain't fancy, but in my store I've got an extra office with a desk that's not bein' used. We'd just need to sweep up and dust. Why, you could use that at no cost. Matter-a-fact, we could fix up a sign out front—paint it red, white, and blue—so the whole town would know your business here."

"Surely, sir, it is by stroke of divine providence that you were at the train station at the exact time when your country needed you. If just a portion of your spirit is found in the people of this nation, there can be no doubt about the outcome of this conflict."

While Rebecca Dye prepared the guest room, Spencer drove Sergeant Burns around town to meet influential citizens—or at least the ones who fell into that category in Spencer's mind. Mayor Melander Dendy offered to make the entire city hall available for the War Department if needed. Three of the five town council members requested the privilege of being the first resident of Hampton Falls to buy war bonds. The other two, who Spencer assumed were closet America Firsters, simply offered their best wishes. Pastor James Darst invited the Sergeant to address the congregation of his church after the New Year's Day service, an invitation that Sergeant Burns humbly accepted.

Spencer, Rebecca, and Isaiah Blassingame, Spencer's hired hand at the store, spent most of New Year's Eve cleaning Sergeant Burns' new office space and making the hardware store presentable. In the front window, they hung patriotic bunting borrowed from the city hall's Fourth of July decorations. Spencer took a 3 x 6 piece of plywood, painted it white, and then stenciled upon it in block letters, "U.S. Army

Recruiting Post: War Bonds for Sale." He attached the finished sign to a sawhorse and placed it in front of the store. The Dyes understood that after the service on New Year's Day, Sergeant Burns would open the post for business.

In the meantime, the Sergeant was made welcome around town—especially by the ladies. Several eyebrows were raised at the amount of time he spent with Eskew Alley's twin girls, Amanda Lee and Bonnie Jean. Based on their conduct, they would forever be known in Hampton Falls as the Alley Cats. The more progressive members of the community believed that the girls were just being patriotic. After all, they were much like the accruements of the Fourth of July, such as fireworks exploding in the night sky and Old Glory fluttering stiffly in the breeze.

News spread quickly around town about the Sergeant and his speaking engagement at Reedy Fork Baptist Church. Once the New Year finally arrived, excitement reached such a level that many of the townspeople showed up an hour before the service just to secure a seat. To his credit, Pastor Darst understood who was the featured attraction of the evening. He gave an abbreviated sermon and chose hymns with a patriotic flavor to prepare the congregation for the Sergeant's oration. And what an oration it was.

As soon as the service closed with "God Bless America," Sergeant Burns ascended the steps, shook Pastor Darst's hand, and looked out over the congregation from the pulpit. Not a space was vacant in the pews. About two dozen men and boys lined the walls, having given up their seats to the fairer sex.

"Ladies and Gentlemen," the Sergeant began, "on behalf of the War Department, I thank you for the kindness you have shown me since I arrived but a few days ago. You have opened your homes to me, given your time, and offered your prayers. I can only hope that the other War Department representatives undertaking my task in various towns throughout the United States have met with one tenth the hospitality and patriotic sentiment that I have." He paused. In those brief seconds of silence, Sergeant Burns' olive eyes panned the room and somehow made contact with the eyes of every man, woman, and child.

"Of course, the war that presses in upon us will require much more than sentiment. Action is needed on the part of our people." The thud from his fist striking the lectern echoed across the sanctuary.

"Only action can preserve our most sacred institutions from the slavery and degradation that the Axis powers seek to foist upon us. Their success in the conflict would mark an end to our way of life and the liberty we too often take for granted.

"Trust that Government officials are, on this very day, working around the clock to mobilize men and materiel for a successful prosecution of the war. These dedicated servants, however, can only work with the resources that they have. As we stand in the dawn of 1942, we must recognize that the resources available are insufficient. It is up to the people of this country to determine whether they will provide what is needed. They must decide whether the Great Experiment in self-government, begun in 1789, is worth the service of their sons and the dedication of their earthly treasures."

Sergeant Burns then discoursed on the bleak situation that General Washington and his troops suffered at Valley Forge in the winter of 1777–78. The avarice of the states, he asserted, in not fulfilling Congress' requisitions, resulted in the Continental Army's having little food, tattered uniforms, and inadequate housing. Unless immediate action was taken, our military could find itself in similar conditions.

"Do you think that the Japanese and Germans are withholding anything that would compromise the fighting ability of their men?" Sergeant Burns asked as he gripped the lectern all the tighter. "If those people, in pursuit of conquest and darkness, will give their all, then what must we do in pursuit of liberty and light?"

The dogged isolationism of the likes of Senator Robert Taft of Ohio, Col. McCormick's *Chicago Tribune*, and Charles Lindbergh had put the nation's military at a disadvantage, the Sergeant explained. "But perhaps the most damaging venom has been spewed by a once gallant military officer in his screed against his country." Everyone in the church knew that he was referring to General Smedley D. Butler's booklet *War Is a Racket*, in which the Medal of Honor winner argued that armed conflict is principally conducted for the benefit of a few con men at the expense of the many. The condensed version that appeared in *Reader's Digest* had made the rounds of the town. Prior to Pearl Harbor, it had been endorsed by many of Hampton Falls' denizens.

As he brought the oration to a close, Sergeant Burns announced that at nine o'clock the next morning he would be at Dye's Hardware Store. He invited the town's young men to drop by and ask any questions they had about enlistment and service. For those unable to bear arms, he offered the chance to purchase war bonds in denominations ranging from $25 to $10,000. They could be purchased, Sergeant Burns explained, at 75 percent of their face value and would earn a 2.9 percent return after a ten-year maturity. In light of the stakes of the contest, the Sergeant questioned whether there was any better investment on the earth.

The next day, when Spencer drove Sergeant Burns to the hardware store, they encountered a line of people on Main Street waiting to perform their patriotic duty. Throughout the day, Spencer's store teemed with activity. Spencer pretended to be going about his normal business and routine but strained to hear the conversations taking place in the spare office. Multiple times that day he overheard the Sergeant explaining the rigors of boot camp, specialized training programs, and estimated times from enlistment to deployment. He heard the Sergeant recording the age, height, and weight of the prospective recruits. After obtaining the recruit's mailing address, the Sergeant would say, "Now, in 10 to 14 days you will receive a letter in the mail instructing you on your report date and mode of transportation. Expect to be starting boot camp before January comes to a close. On behalf of a grateful nation, I thank you."

In Spencer's estimation, bond sales far outpaced the enlistments. The Sergeant commandeered the store's portable Underwood typewriter and used it to inscribe each purchaser's name and address on the bonds. Sergeant Burns was a gifted salesman. More than once, Spencer heard his efficacious pitch. "How gracious you are to purchase a $25 bond. This will provide one of our soldiers with basic training. But with a $50 bond, which will cost you a mere $37.50, you can fill his ammunition pouches—and just maybe one of those bullets will have Herr Hitler's name on it. Can I count on you for this?" Inevitably, Spencer then would hear the Sergeant exclaim, "I knew I could!" or "You just run to the bank, and I'll be right here."

Patriotic fervor, however, boiled over and caused an incident at Dr. Cecil T. Sandifer's house. The entire town knew that the good doctor was a member of the America First Committee. Prior to Pearl Harbor, Dr. Sandifer made no bones about his belief that the Roosevelt administration was conspiring to provoke a foreign war. Sergeant Burns' new enlistees, after toasting themselves with a jug of Winston Price's white lightnin', held their first drill in front of the Sandifer residence and burned the doctor in effigy. Words were exchanged, and multiple rocks, propelled at a high rate of speed, met the glass of Dr. Sandifer's exterior windows.

The Sergeant continued to conduct business for the next several days. The number of people coming to the hardware store eventually returned to its pre-New Year's levels. At that point, Sergeant Burns explained to the Dyes that his mission in Hampton Falls was accomplished, and that it was time for him to move to his next assignment. "My time here has been a true blessing," the Sergeant averred. "Any concerns I previously had about the spirit of the American people have been dispelled. No matter where fate might have me stationed in the coming months and years, I will be able to think back on my visit here and put into perspective just who and what I am fighting for."

The next day Spencer dropped off Sergeant Burns at the train station. Spencer queried about the Sergeant's next destination, but the Sergeant politely explained that he was not at liberty to disclose such information, and that civilians should get accustomed to keeping quiet about *any* troop movements or deployments. Spencer nodded. "Loose lips sink ships," he proclaimed.

Once back at the shop, Spencer tried to reclaim his former routine. He decided he would leave the bunting up just one more day. Spencer could not help but feeling pride about his role in hosting Sergeant Burns and the whole town's associating Dye's Hardware with the war effort.

Spencer fumbled under the main counter and located a small picture frame. He loosened the back panel and laid the frame face down. He then retrieved the $25 war bond that he had purchased the day after the Sunday oration. The bond was crisp and on the left side was a portrait with an inscription underneath that read "Geo. Washington." In a move of tactical brilliance, Spencer had given Burns the money at the height of the first day's business and sent Isaiah into the office to retrieve the bond, thereby preempting the Sergeant's opportunity to give him the ammo pouch plea.

Although this was not the actual first bond purchased from Sergeant Burns, Spencer figured that, constructively, it was, inasmuch as he had provided free living quarters and office space to the War Department. Hence, he was entitled to claim this honor.

Spencer carefully placed the bond into the frame, reattached the back panel, and hung the bond on his wall just behind the cash register. He beamed as he imagined Dr. Sandifer slinking into the store and his eyes coming to rest on this emblem of patriotism—the first war bond purchased in Hampton Falls.

Spencer walked around to the front of the counter and stood in the place where he imagined that Dr. Sandifer would be mumbling about war being a racket. Spencer studied the bond and remembered the Sergeant's moving description of George Washington's men at Valley Forge. Spencer figured that the portrait of Washington on the bond must have been done while the General and his men struggled in their winter quarters. That would explain the beard, Spencer reasoned, because he had not recalled ever seeing a portrait of Washington with facial hair.

Christopher Farris

Two Kinds of People

Specialist Hawkins huddled under his poncho, kept his cigarette close to his face, and tried to keep out the damp. The rain fell invisible from the charcoal blackness. It flashed into existence under the hospital's parking lot lights. It poured in waves. It ran across the pavement in lines like marching troops. Frenetic thunder and lightning boomed and flashed like celestial artillery. Heavy gusts blew the torrent sideways under the ER overhang, wetting the bottom of the men's Army uniforms, drenching woodland green knees, slicking black leather boot tips.

The city was a moldering, silent place, invisible from this island of generator powered light. New Orleans had been given over to the rats, the feral dog packs, the gators, the junkies, and the street people. Hawkins was ruminating sourly on how this once beautiful city had been destroyed. He was thinking about how little it took for a thing of quirky beauty to become a complete and dysfunctional hell-hole.

He was bored. It was too wet to study his Officer Candidate Guide. Too wet to run. Too late to call his wife. Too dark to look around. Too freaking everything, everything to do anything, anything. He'd woken with an itch in the back of his throat, sure precursor to a cold. He wanted to be home, in his own Arkansas bed, instead of stuck in Katrina-ravaged New Orleans while Hurricane Rita pounded the Texas shoreline.

Most of the platoon was asleep in the Wellness Center down the street and around the corner. Hawkins and the kid from Tennessee, whom Sergeant Bobby had unaccountably taken to calling Shaboom, were the only two soldiers standing guard in front of the ER door.

"No point in all of us bein' miserable," Bobby'd said. The sergeant had carefully finished the daily sharpening of his grandfather's hunting knife, wrapped knife and sheath in an oilcloth carefully, and then set up a rotation with minimal staffing for the night.

The big sergeant had left Hawkins in charge and had run through puddles to the hospice building across the hospital parking lot. All of the hospice's pre-hurricane residents were dead and stored in the hospital's morgue, awaiting a continually postponed burial. The darkened building had been converted to temporary housing for the volunteer nurses. The hospice/nurses' residence was off limits to everyone but Bobby and, when Bobby needed collecting, Hawkins.

Hawkins expected the sergeant would get wasted tonight. Bobby's wife still wasn't answering or returning his calls. His big friend had begun to doubt whether he had a home to return to. Hawkins had his own family troubles, but he didn't think he had that particular worry, not yet, at least. Hawkins figured Bobby was deep into the nursing staff's liquor by now, his six-foot-seven self draped around a compliant woman that the sergeant had befriended. Only God knew what kind of meds the man was popping or in what quantity. The shrinks had been generous after Iraq. Quiet night, big storm, broken home—Bobby was partying it all away.

Hawkins groaned and grumbled but picked up the slack for his big friend, tried to calm his own anxieties. When they'd arrived in this great waterlogged city, they'd talked of opening a movie theater for kids on the Oklahoma border, of going it civilian and sober, away from constant deployments, free from fifteen-hour days and asshole Commanders. They'd promised to play this thing straight. Bobby was breaking that promise and a long list of regulations as well.

Hawkins was tired. There had been too many overgrown neighborhoods, too many dogs to shoot, too many ringworm decorated junkies, and far too many racist cops who laughed about what they did to looters, all the while filling the backseats of their cruisers with stolen electronics. There had been far, far too many dead bodies. Part of Hawkins wanted to be in the hospice drinking it all away just like his buddy, Bobby. The other part was just glad the man wasn't under the shelter with him.

Something had changed with Bobby. Something had gone wrong. His friend had had one too many tours of duty, had become unpredictable and violent, apt to weep uncontrollably one minute and rage over small infractions the next. Bobby seemed to be coming apart at the edges, and this deployment, right after a stint in an Army psych ward, was accelerating the process. Hawkins had wondered who the genius was that thought it was a good idea to send a broken soldier, freshly court-martialed for battery of a superior officer and looting Iraqi war dead, to protect civilians in New Orleans. No one in the chain of command seemed to want to take responsibility for the decision, but that hadn't stopped them from making Hawkins responsible for Bobby's behavior. He was just praying he could hold the big man together until they boarded the C130 for home.

Hawkins kept glancing nervously through the glass walls of the ER, hoping not to see the hospital's private military contractor, Hammer. The dude was built like a fireplug, uniformed himself in black, and wore a Sam Brown belt with lots of ornamental gear, cuffs, and sprays. He carried a pistol right on his hip. He was a man that liked to signify. Hammer was an ex-Marine with an alpha dog personality, just like Bobby. As soon as they'd met, the two men had taken to snorting and sniffing around each other. Bobby and Hammer were looking for reasons to hate each other. Hawkins had known immediately that it was going to end badly.

Hammer had made it clear that the Army guys, meaning Bobby's crew, weren't allowed in the ER or the hospital, that they could protect the parking lot and the FEMA people camped there. None of them, he said, were welcome inside. Even to use the bathroom. The presence of the female hospital staff seemed to ramp up his aggression. He had a point to prove. Bobby shrugged and frowned, and Hawkins, who could see through the nonchalance, moved to a position where he could interpose himself between the two men if needed. Hammer noticed and smiled.

Bobby's silence encouraged the contractor, who began loudly questioning why the perplexed soldiers were in New Orleans instead of doing their job "killin' Iraqis in the sandbox." Were they just the second-string soldiers nobody could get any use out of? Hawkins had tried to laugh it off but gnawed his fingers instead. He knew Bobby couldn't take that kind of provocation. He was right. Bobby had stopped idly looking around and fixed Hammer with a strange look. He had made a troublesome motion with his lips, almost a smile. Not quite.

"Goddam, son," Bobby had said to Hammer and shook out his arms, rolled his shoulders, his neck, "I heard some news about you Blackwater fellas. I hear ya'll are some real high-speed soldier-types. They said ya'll got your asses hung from an Iraqi bridge. Hung! That's pretty hard to imagine for a guy like me. I done spent three tours in Iraq, hell, I been in every conflict since 1989, and ain't none of my guys have nothing like that go down. What happened? Ya'll forget you had rifles? How many of ya'll they kill? Three? Four? Dumb-asses. Ya'll must've looked mighty ornamental hanging there in those pretty outfits."

Bobby'd popped his lips at Hammer, gave him his trademark sneer. He'd picked his great apish teeth at the man and watched him out of the corner of his eye. Hammer's face had gone red with anger and embarrassment, but Bobby'd pretended not to notice. Hawkins figured it was about to go off, but strangely, Hammer, though grievously provoked, let it lie. Hawkins couldn't figure out why. He thought maybe the guard had recognized that Bobby wasn't playing by the rules anymore, wasn't tracking reality too well. Maybe Hammer had just had a bad premonition or something. Whatever the reason, the guard left the tension to simmer.

Later that night, a woman was brought in by her panicked husband. A starving Rottweiler had turned her forearm into a mess of weeping red meat. Hawkins could have put his hand between the tongue-like loop of the woman's dangling muscle, still attached at wrist and elbow, and her exposed twiggy forearm bones. Hammer had tried to turn her away to the FEMA folks camped in the parking lot. The hospital had been refusing patients unless FEMA promised to pay. Hawkins didn't understand the problem or the politics, but he did know the FEMA folks weren't equipped to deal with anything this serious. The fainting woman and the blood on the pavement had been all the excuse Bobby needed to start the postponed fight. It had taken Hawkins and four of his soldiers to get the sergeant and the ex-marine separated. Thank God, a doctor with some common sense had ushered the woman into the ER while the security details were tussling.

After the fight, Hammer stood, arms-crossed and chin-tucked, inside the ER, glowering while Bobby walked a loose-limbed, prowling circle in front of the thick ER glass. Hawkins had stood an uncertain guard between the two, his rifle across his chest. Bobby's resemblance to a rabid dog might have been comical if Hawkins hadn't known how close the man was to completely losing it.

No, Hawkins didn't enjoy standing out in the rain in the middle of the night, but, all things considered, he was damned glad Bobby was staying away. Hawkins and Bobby's tour of duty ended in two days. *Better wet and miserable*, he thought, *than to have another incident.*

*

0200 saw a slowing of the rain and a set of headlights, high and wide, approaching down the distant street in front of the boarded-up liquor store. A lightning flash showed a large, long, bread-box-like shape. A bus maybe. Tour or school. Hawkins couldn't tell.

Shitty night to be on tour, he thought.

It rolled slowly down the street, the great diesel engine rumbling.

Definitely a tour bus. What's it doing out here?

The body was black, long dark windows down the side, brushed aluminum wheels. HARLOW TOURS was painted on the side in great white letters. It seemed to hesitate at the stop sign on the corner, sniffed around like a lost dog, then nosed across the empty street and followed the signs to the ambulance circle. It entered the cul-de-sac from the wrong direction and squealed to a hesitant stop.

Hawkins motioned for Shaboom to stay where he was, walked out from the overhang. The rain pounded on the hood of his poncho, splashed into his eyes. He saw the driver through the front window. The man's face reflected the sickly green of his dashboard lights. The driver was pressing buttons on the dash, his face set in a grimace that looked like panic.

The great vehicle's air brakes released with a hiss; Hawkins knocked on the glass of the bus's door impatiently. He hunched forward and tried to keep his weapon under the edge of his poncho, keep it as dry as possible.

Hurry up, man, he thought, *it's wet out here.*

The door ground open. The driver rose partially from his seat, eyes wide, face dismayed.

"They taking people here?" he asked.

There was an odd quaver in his voice. A hope. Panic.

"Yeah," Hawkins replied. "But you're going to have to move your bus. You're blocking the ambulance lane."

Hawkins climbed the steps into the bus. His rifle barrel banged against the rubber molding. His poncho streamed rain onto the steps. The stink of stale urine swept over him. Made him gag. He raised his hand to nose and mouth.

"Good God," he said, "What's that smell?"

The heat inside the bus was stifling, jungle-like and oppressive. It smelled of garbage, of medicine, and unwashed bodies.

"Look, man," the driver's face was stretched with horror, his words running over themselves. He waved his hand to the rear of the bus "I got all these old people. I gotta put 'em someplace. I need help."

Hawkins took another step up the stairs and looked into the rear of the bus. The overhead track-lighting was out, but occasional lightning illuminated the interior. Elderly people in robes, pajamas, some in hospital gowns or thin blankets, occupied the front rows of seats. There was a naked man in the fourth aisle, his chest mushroom-white and striped with the shadows of his ribs. White-haired heads lolled against seat backs. Some slumped forward over their own laps. He could see where they had vomited in the aisles, on themselves. Trash and feces littered the center carpet runner. The rear rows of seats had been removed, medical beds strapped in place. More bodies lay under white sheets, their drawn and vacuous faces exposed in the storm flashes.

Hawkins's eyes froze for a moment on a woman in the third row. Her tongue looked like a dry sponge shoved between her grey lips. A fly was lighting on her forehead, cheek, left eyeball. Her eyes were open. Glazed. The woman's face was putty-like and gelid.

"Jesus," Hawkins gasped. "Is she dead?"

"Yeah, man," the driver choked. "Yeah, man. That's what I'm saying. She's dead and others, I got lots of— This hospital open or not?"

"What—what?" Hawkins's mind was stuttering.

"We evacuated from Houston, man. Air-conditioner gave out about halfway, then we got separated from the lead vehicle a ways back. All the gas stations are closed, I can't make a phone call. I didn't know what else to do. They've been dying. I've just been driving and they've been dying. I—I—They've been dying! Please help me! Please!"

"Jesus," Hawkins said, tripped on the bottom step, fell off the bus backwards, and sprawled onto the concrete. The bus driver followed him out.

Hawkins pushed himself to his feet in the slow rain and grabbed the man by his arm, pulled him toward the hospital.

"You evacuated from Houston to New Orleans?" he shouted, "Are you f— Are you crazy?"

The driver didn't answer, simply dipped his head and hurried under the ER overhang. Hawkins, rushing after, suddenly stopped.

Hammer stood outside the ER entrance. The security guard was playing with a collapsible police baton. Holding it in his hand and extending it with a flip of the wrist, then pushing it closed against his stomach. The big man stared at the tour bus with a snarl on his face. Hawkins groaned and looked to Shaboom for support. The young soldier's eyes were pinned to Hammer, and he had backed almost all the way out into the rain. The kid jumped when a soggy palm frond brushed the side of his cheek. Shaboom was terrified of Hammer. No help there.

Dammit, Hawkins thought.

"Go get Dr. Adams. Now!"

Shaboom didn't ask any questions. The young soldier gave Hammer a final worried look and disappeared across the parking lot, heading for the FEMA tents and the senior government doctor. The skies opened up afresh and a shower of lightning flashed down. A deep rumble of thunder shook the concrete under their feet.

"Hammer," Hawkins said desperately, "these folks need help. Now. Right now!"

He kept walking forward. Hoping against hope that the security contractor would move out of his way.

"What they need," Hammer replied with a scowl, moving to put himself between Hawkins and the door, "is to go through the FEMA team like they're supposed to."

He made a rapid movement with his right hand. The baton popped open with a metallic click. He slammed it closed with his left hand. Hammer's eyes never left Hawkins's face.

"How many times I gotta tell you losers," Hammer asked, "before you get it right? All patients go through the FEMA team before the hospital."

"Look, man—" Hawkins began desperately.

The bus driver sheltered behind Hawkins's shoulder. His eyes swiveled between the two men rapidly. The driver looked like a man who couldn't figure what the hell was happening and how to make it stop.

"I ain't your man," Hammer snapped. "Why don't you go get your sergeant? I ain't dealing with no hopped-up private."

Hawkins, on the edge of panic, felt a slow burn start in his head. Tried to hold on to reason.

"Alright, Hammer," he said as calmly as he could manage. "There are dead people on that bus, and—"

"Bullshit," the security guard interrupted calmly. Hawkins stopped. His mouth hung open.

"Whaddya mean bullshit?" he replied. "They're dead!"

The driver behind him made a small noise in his throat.

"I mean, Private." Hammer leaned forward, thrust his meaty chin in Hawkins's face. "Bull. Shit!"

Thunder sounded again, coming nearer. The rain made a drumming sound on the pavement. Drumming. Drumming.

Hawkins's hands made futile gestures, he searched for the words that would get through Hammer's intransigence. The guard had a smirk on his face. He was enjoying his power, his petty revenge. Hawkins's anger kicked up a notch. He thought about a fly landing on a still, glassy eye. He looked around wildly, hoping for Dr. Adams to come running out of the rain to solve the problem. No luck. He tried speaking again.

"I've seen them, Hammer," he said as calmly as he could. "The bus driver will confirm it. There are dead people on that bus and—"

"And I say bullshit," Hammer interrupted.

"And more dying!" Hawkins yelled.

"You guys wouldn't know a dead person if it slapped ya in the face," Hammer sneered. "You just think you're too good to follow procedures. Just like your buddy, Bobby. Well, I'm telling you now; I had a talk with the hospital administrator after you fellas tried to get me in trouble last time, and he ain't taking any patients without insurance until they been through the feds. So, unless somebody's bleeding out, they go through the FEMA tents first. First!"

"Dammit, Hammer, the feds aren't equipped to deal with this. They're dying. I'm telling you—" Hawkins said.

"Anybody bleeding?!" Hammer interrupted.

Hawkins shook his head in disbelief. Reality was out of kilter, someone had changed the rules of the world on him. He could see sanity on the other side of the ER's glassed vestibule, could see the gathered doctors and nurses pointing at him and Hammer, watching their confrontation, but he couldn't get to them. He couldn't get past Hammer. There was too much hate in the man's face.

"If they ain't bleeding out, they go through the FEMA tent," Hammer repeated. "I already told you that, twelve fuckin' times!" He paused, wild-eyed, then went on in a tight voice. "So get your ass over to the FEMA tent and—" he gestured with the opened baton to the bus driver behind Hawkins's shoulder. "You, you get your fuckin' bus out a' my ambulance lane! Pronto!"

Hawkins gestured again, pleading with open hands, wordless.

"Besides," Hammer continued, "if they're really dead, then it ain't no emergency. Now is it?"

The bus driver gave a low despairing groan that Hawkins barely heard. Something had gone white-hot behind Hawkins's brow. He lunged around Hammer in a wild attempt to get through the ER doors, trying to reach someone who would listen, someone who was sane.

Pain exploded in his right temple where Hammer struck him with the baton. Hawkins felt himself on his hands and knees on the pavement. His rifle, fallen from his grip, tumbled across the pavement and out into the rain-drenched dark.

"Jesus man! Jesus man! Jesus man! Jesus man!" the bus driver repeated in a high voice.

The words registered small and distant in Hawkins's ears. He shook his head, trying to clear the pain, and looked up. Hammer stood over him triumphantly, baton raised for another strike. The big man's mouth opened to shriek something, something horrible, as he struck again.

Hawkins lunged off the pavement. He wrapped his arms around

the contractor's waist and barreled the man backwards against a portico pillar. Pure joy plunged through his veins, and the pain in his skull was forgotten. He was scared. He was furious. Hammer's breath left his body in a hot gust. They struggled briefly against the pillar until Hammer regained his balance. The thick man struck down on Hawkins's shoulders with a closed fist and the heavy baton, each battering blow driving the soldier lower and lower toward the pavement.

Hawkins shook his muzzy head, growling like an animal, and whipped a fist into his attacker's stomach. He felt Hammer's paunch give under his knuckles, heard Hammer groan as a rib gave. Hawkins staggered back and struck out again, this time square on Hammer's chin. He didn't feel the blow contact. He hardly felt anything at all.

Hammer grunted and his eyes went dim for a moment, his lip drooped, bovine and slack, but then he gathered himself. The baton went up again and then down. The lead tip ricocheted off Hawkins's temple, tore at his ear, and struck him squarely on the shoulder. Blackness exploded behind his eyes and he went to one knee. Blood trickled down his eye ridge, caught in his eyelashes. Hammer stepped back to swing a final time. Hawkins tried to raise his arms in defense.

From behind Hawkins, the sound of heavy, rushing boots came from the darkness. Sergeant Bobby, tall and streaming with water, came from the storm, silent, fast and low, his grandfather's hunting knife in his hand. The sergeant flashed through Hawkins's dazed vision, drove Hammer up and back against the thick glass walls of the ER waiting room. The glass shuddered with the impact of the two large bodies.

Hammer gave out a great whooshing, "Phawwwwffff." Sergeant Bobby's knife was going back and forth, plunging over and over and over again into Hammer's stomach. Striking home and pulling back. Striking home. Hammer made sounds. Sounds that sounded like a punctured tire deflating. A gasped wheeeeeeeeee repeated, and still Bobby's arm went back and forth like a machine, the blade plunging in and out of the guard's stomach.

Bobby was growling now. Howling in wolfen rage. Hawkins staggered upright and lunged. He knocked Bobby away from Hammer.

"No!" he cried at the sergeant.

Hawkins half fell, half drove Bobby to the pavement. Bobby was grunting under him. Pushing against Hawkins. Pounding him. Hawkins felt the blade enter his stomach, once, twice, felt it probing around inside. His eyes went wide with pain and fright. He felt the sudden need to vomit but didn't.

"Bobby!" Hawkins cried. "Bobby! Bobby! Stop!"

Sergeant Bobby slumped under his grip. His mad eyes closed. Body shuddering. Taking in great drafts of air. The big sergeant's blood-drenched hunting knife fell from his hand.

Hawkins rolled onto his back painfully, groaned, and forced himself to sit up. His belly was on fire. Something shifted inside.

Hammer slid bonelessly down the glass wall, a hand on his barrel belly, eyes wide with disbelief and shock. The man's blood-soaked t-shirt clung to his belly. The guard took short, sharp breaths.

Whee. Whee. Whee.

The bus driver stood nervously to the side, turning first toward the hospital, then toward the bus, too terrified to take a step either way.

"Go!" Hawkins croaked at the driver. "Go get help! Now!"

The man stared at him for another moment. Not comprehending.

"Now!" Hawkins shrieked, wincing at the sharp pain in his head and stomach.

The driver ran into the hospital with a scream that started as a low groan and rose as he passed through the ER doors. Hawkins turned back to Bobby. The big man's eyes were closed tight like a child trying to unsee something. His face was a study in misery. The big sergeant began to shudder. Sobbing.

"I wished we'd opened that theater," Bobby groaned. "I wished I'd gotten out of the Army. I wished I wasn't ever here. I just wanted to open a theater."

His voice trailed off into sobbing. Shaking shoulders. He wiped his eyes with his hands. Roughly. One hand left a red streak across his cheek, cupped his mouth. The sergeant wept quietly through gritted teeth and clenched fingers. He was holding it in as best as he could.

Hawkins reached over and put his hand on the big man's chest. He wanted to tell his friend that they still could. That it'd be the best damn kid's theater ever. That everything would be alright. That this could be fixed. That his wife would take him back. That they'd get him help at the VA. That his kids would love him again.

The words stuck in Hawkins's throat. He choked on them. Sobbed. He couldn't get them out. He knew they weren't true. Tears tracked silent down Hawkins's cheeks. He began to shake as well. He was suddenly cold. He felt himself spilling out, falling away.

"My granddaddy," Bobby said faintly, "said they wasn't but two kinds a' people in the world. Cowards and bullies, and heroes. I . . . wanted to be a hero."

Hawkins heard sirens in the distance. They were coming closer. He slumped beside Bobby. The sergeant lay on the cement, a great arm across his brow, feet splayed and drooped in despair. Hawkins looked back at Hammer. The guard breathed hard, jerking in short breaths. The hospital staff surrounded him. Lifted him to a crash cart and wheeled the dying man into the ER.

The scene jumped every time Hawkins changed his focus. The world became a series of frozen vignettes that did not exist until he turned eyes upon it. Flash, Hammer bleeding. Flash, the lights on inside the bus. Flash, Dr. Adams standing over him, her mouth agape. Flash, the bodies on gurneys rolling out of the rain. The world ceased to exist when he looked away. He felt unutterably weary. Jangled. He couldn't decide what to do. Move, don't move. He simply patted Bobby on the shoulder over and over again. Pushed his other palm against the puncture wounds in his own stomach. Felt the hot blood running between his fingers. Into his lap.

Hawkins thought about his mom, his wife, his children. He suddenly felt stupid, vastly foolish. He'd volunteered for this duty against his wife's wishes. Now, he had a deep desire to go home, to have never left. He wanted to hold and to be held, to smell the familiar scent of his wife's hair and to touch his children's hands. He wanted to hear the gravel of his father's voice. Hawkins repeated faintly, "It'll be alright. It'll be alright. It'll be alright," and patted his friend's chest like a lost and fearful child. "It'll be alright."

Garlen Wayne Funnell
How To Become a USMC Selected Toy

Hello, I am a GI JOE USMC Gunner in Vietnam. Today I started out in the Mattel Toy Development Project or MTDD. I have been selected to be a Vietnam USMC gunner. I have my M60 machine gun, two machine-gun belts, a .45 cal pistol, my camouflage helmet, jungle boots, dark blended, light green jungle utilities, two canteens, a red battle dressing high on my right arm, painted black beard, a tripod, flak jacket, a PRC-25 radio (short range radio), and my 782 gear.

Now I wonder who I was made after. I saw my tag, Hill 488. I was based on Hill 488 personnel in the Republic of South Vietnam, June 23, 1967. I was awarded the Medal of Honor, based on the full NVA attack. I ran out of ammo, so I threw rocks. Nobody was spared a wound that night.

But where do I go now? Yes, I am going to a Vietnam diorama, to be on display, to recall the glory and fighting of Hill 488. The kids look at me with open mouths, grasping and hooting. But the grownups, looking with a tear or two in their eyes, are remembering a faraway place. Yes, today is a good day for a good day.

Monty Joynes
No Medals, Please

Fate is a crooked dealer of cards. The Army drafted me when I failed to keep up my hours in graduate school. I was drowning in the mediocrity of a master's degree in clinical psychology. I made the mistake of telling the head of the department that his curriculum was full of shit. As a dangerously frustrated twenty-five-year-old who had already dropped out of the mainstream for a dreadful year, I was almost relieved when I got my draft notice.

I actually enjoyed Basic Training at Fort Gordon, Georgia. I was so old compared to the eighteen and nineteen year olds that they called me "Pop." I was often invited to sign up for Officer Candidate School, but I preferred to be a grunt and limit my military experience to two years. At that time, I considered the Army as my own personal laboratory for the study of behavioral modification.

I was near the top of my medical corpsman class. I was an expert rifle shot, and I was older and more mature than the other shaved heads. When the training company commander ordered me to present myself in summer Class-A uniform to some major at battalion headquarters, I thought it would be another pitch to become an officer. What was offered was quite different. They were looking for a medic to join a special team. I would have to go through Advanced Infantry Training, the Fort Bragg Jump School, and, surviving that, undergo additional field training with the special unit before being assigned to a mission.

"What's the job, sir?" I asked. "What does the special team do?"

The major looked for me to blink when he replied, "Assassination and kidnap."

I smiled the smile I had perfected by studying the films of Henry Fonda, the kind of smile that unnerves a bar fighter who has just threatened to bite your head off and spit out your eyeballs. The smile says, "Okay. What else?"

There is still the 1947 National Security Act resulting from WW II that prevents me from being more specific in detailing the next eighteen months. I might even be subject to imprisonment for what I have disclosed thus far. But this is not a story about warfare.

I learned the down and dirty of my business at a special training camp in the jungles of Thailand. Anyway, somebody said it was Thailand. All I saw was an airport tarmac where I lugged my duffel bag the length of a football field from a C-130 to a Huey helicopter. I saw no temples or any exotic dancers with long fingernails.

The jungle training was more severe than the stateside hell of AIT or Airborne. I didn't think I had any weight left to lose, but I dropped another eleven pounds. I was killed enough times by booby traps planted along a trail that I began to sense trip wires without seeing them. The instructors punished us until we were instinctual jungle animals. We learned to be more terrible than the insects, snakes, or enemy that we might have feared.

My main responsibility was to keep the team medically fit. That is not a simple task when you're running a clandestine jungle operation. I got intense instruction from a doctor on all the fevers, parasites, and skin diseases of the region, plus an eight-day side trip to a combat area in Vietnam, where I had my first look at traumatic casualties. A triage officer taught me the basics of who lives and who dies from gunshot and shrapnel wounds. I would have to advise the mission CO when a member of our team was too far gone to evacuate. The decision had an edge on it as hard and as sharp as a commando knife.

No one ever said, "You graduated." One day I turned in all my uniforms, gear, and identification, and took on foreign camouflage fatigues, very expensive boots with rubber bottoms, and an assortment of weapons I had never learned to fire. A couple of weeks later, I could break down and clean each piece inside a black bag and fire them at expert levels, with or without silencers.

I got three days off to sleep. It was enough healing time for the abrasions, insect welts, and leech scars of the previous twelve weeks. Then I was assigned to a nine-man team. Nothing but a body bag could separate us. We married each other the moment we met. For better or worse, till death do us part. Nine bush rats with a mean and ugly future.

The captain who led our team was a "Ranger." Rangers were more elite than Green Berets. I guess I was a Ranger, too, by the time I completed training, but nobody offered me the insignia. We called the captain "Boss." He was a tall, wiry man who didn't waste words or energy. He was a Bible reader, believe it or not, and probably had a family. Most of what we learned about him was professional. He was an exceedingly meticulous planner. He was bush smart and very decisive. I don't ever remember questioning his judgment. His skill in managing extremely dangerous situations still seems as miraculous to me now as it did then. With nearly forty missions over a fourteen-month period, we lost no members of our team and very few of the Vietnamese agents who worked with us.

"Top" was the senior NCO and the man in charge of general operations. He also had a Ranger background and had been a young

Pathfinder in Korea. He participated in the only Airborne assault of that entire war. He was a burly warhorse with a firm mouth and jaw. He was in his mid-thirties and was already showing grey in his hair, but he seemed to have the physical endurance and strength of five men— even five as tough as we thought we were. He was a merciless training instructor who often pushed you until you hated him. On the other hand, he was a pushover when it came to off-duty high jinks. He was, for example, a key man in scrounging the building materials for our club and stood the first round of drinks when Diamond Tim installed the stolen furniture.

"Uncle" was next in the chain of command. He was our intelligence and language specialist, although he looked more like a college professor than a soldier. Uncle carried a grin on his face that implied he was satisfied with whatever happened. He once talked to me about Zen and the use of meditation to control emotions. I missed the message and undervalued what he had to teach me. It took me fifteen years to get to the place he was already coming from. That's the wisdom of retrospect. But even then, all of us respected Uncle and realized that he had to do his job well if we were to survive. He worked with the shadowy intelligence network that set up our targets. He not only spoke Vietnamese, but he also seemed to be able to think like they did in tactical situations. Behind enemy lines, Boss and Top depended on Uncle to call the hard shots.

Uncle's uniform seemed to swallow him. If he was thin, he was not frail. He toted his weight just like the rest of us, and demonstrated his ability and willingness to kill when necessary. If we felt that Uncle was distant, it was only because he would not join us in our tension relieving horseplay and marathon drinking sessions. Uncle may have enjoyed being mysterious.

"Radio" was our communications specialist. He not only had to haul a big load, but he also had to protect it as our lifeline to air support and escape. Radio had been recruited from the 82nd Airborne. He was no kid. This was his second tour of Nam. He didn't seem to have much formal education, but communications equipment loved him. A device that would work for no one else would change from static to four-by-four in his hands.

Out in the bush, Radio was a stoic protective shadow to the Boss. He had a very powerful upper body and a vise-like grip that he sometimes used to get your attention if you were not showing appropriate respect to his equipment. Radio also displayed a tendency toward meanness. When left out of an ambush, he was not above adding a few rounds from his seldom-fired pistol into the already dead bodies.

The explosives expert on our team was called "Wires." He was a career Army man, a redhead from Virginia, who was good company. Easy to laugh and swap a story right in the middle of any foolishness one of us could invent, Wires was the most popular member of our team. Wires was also respected. He was my back-up on the medic bag, and he was abundantly proficient in the field. He laid the claymore booby traps that covered our rear and protected our flanks. He often got close enough to the enemy to smell the cooking. For such a fun-loving guy, Wires could be a cool, cool operator.

"Fixer" was our weapons expert. He was another professional soldier who taught us the drill of our exotic, non-issue rifles, machine guns, and pistols. Fixer had loved and collected guns since his early teens. Being paid to work with his choice of the best hardware in the world gave him more pleasure than sex. We never heard him refer to a woman with the passionate affection that he reserved for weapons. Staying straight with Fixer meant paying the appropriate respect to your AK-47, Sten, or Beretta. Asking him to adjust the finger pressure on your trigger was a way of getting anything you wanted from his ditty bag, including a long pull from his last bottle of Jack Daniels.

As good as Fixer was as an instructor and ordnance specialist, he was even better in the field. Killing was merely an exercise to prove the efficiency of his hardware. A Sten gun fires so rapidly that firing a two- or three-round burst is almost impossible for the average soldier. One of the tall tales about Fixer was that he once cut his initials in a tree with a Sten.

Fixer had a deep purple birthmark that spread two palm-lengths across his shoulder and back. He was self-conscious about it and seldom removed his shirt, even among the team members. Fixer also had more moles on his body than anyone I have ever seen. Watching him shave with a straight razor often drew a crowd of thrill seekers.

"Muscles" was the kid on our team. He enlisted after a poor performance in high school. His grades had knocked him off the wrestling team, where he was an undefeated heavyweight, and off the football team, where he had made All-State as a junior. Muscles found a home in the Army and excelled as the leader of an infantry squad. He met Fixer (who was almost old enough to be his father), when he took a small-arms course in foreign weapons. The class of NCOs promoted a shooting contest between Fixer, the instructor, and Muscles, the boy wonder. The match was close enough to earn respect on both sides. When our team was planned, Fixer recommended that Muscles be recruited. The surrogate father-son rivalry continued. They were inseparable in the magnetism of their generation gap. Big, blonde, handsome Muscles and short, ugly Fixer, both in love with the same mistress: killing hardware.

The final member of our team was christened "Spook." Spook was a New Englander who had graduated from Dartmouth and allowed himself to be drafted with much the same malaise that had affected me. He was Uncle's second in intelligence operations. The Army had given him a rocker staff sergeant's stripe to re-enlist after two years. Spook was hooked on his job, curious about Vietnam, and had re-upped to seek adventure in uniform. AIT and Airborne training almost did him in physically. He went from middleweight to lightweight status, but his Yankee pride got him through, and he reported to Thailand in the guise of a tough little S.O.B.

For the first two months together we cross-trained each other and ran three-day escape-and-evasion exercises that were primitive confrontations with survival. A riverboat would drop us in a rainforest as black as an underground sewer, and we would have to get to a pre-determined grid coordinate, which might be a Vietnamese hamlet, and then get ourselves to an LZ in a completely opposite direction. We traveled only at night and covered our trail wherever we passed. We were supposed to be invisible to both the enemy and to friendlies. At night, we could be targets for either. Our missions were never advertised. Getting in and getting out without being detected was the name of the game. These training exercises could get you killed.

When the real missions started, we went with seven of the nine members. Two men served as back-ups and mission support. Everybody got his share of dirty time. Our usual modus operandi was to have an informer lead the target into our kill zone. This was the intelligence side of the mission that made us vulnerable to double agents. The key to the setups was almost always a Vietnamese informant.

If we had to snatch a village chief, for example, we'd try to isolate him in a pre-determined area where we could get away clean. The same setup worked if we were ordered to kill him. Once the ID was made, the target would be hit by two or three men with silenced automatic weapons. Wham! The hollow-point shells would explode on contact and leave the victim almost unrecognizable as a human being. A coup de grace was never required.

The killing was done mostly by Top, Uncle, Fixer, and Muscles. On the first missions, I guarded a flank and saw only the results in a rapid pass as we withdrew. Then we ambushed a party of six, and I was part of the fire team. They were just shadows speaking a foreign tongue against a tropical night. Uncle confirmed the ID, and we cut them down in a pounding of deep, dull thuds, characteristic of the silencers. The shadows collapsed, their talk evaporating into the heat. The insect and animal sounds mixed with our adrenaline-enriched breathing. Boss and Top confirmed the kills beyond my sight. I never saw their faces or their blood. The action was surreal. When it was over, it was like the memory of visiting a shooting gallery where the targets were cartoons, not real people.

In most of the snatch missions, I gave the target a hypo of Thorazine to help his attitude during our escape. I also carried a mystery solution apart from my medical kit that was reserved for terminal putdowns. There was no Army S.O.P. instructing its use—as if we operated as a regular Army unit. We weren't Army. We were bandits. We stole what we could not requisition. When our support gunship pilots could not get aviator gloves for the cold night flying, and we discovered a black-market sidewalk stand full of them in Saigon, we made a quick plan, posted lookouts, and Muscles held the nine millimeter on the merchant while we looted every glove in sight.

Or when we could not get a replacement for the ¾-ton truck that we used to carry ordnance to the gunships, and we saw a fleet of new ones in a South Vietnamese Army depot, we cut the fence, stole a truck, and had new numbers on it before we hit the first checkpoint. Spook even had bogus paperwork for the new truck.

Or when Diamond Tim and his Huey gunship crew looted a beachfront nightclub for its furniture so that our combined Officers-NCO Club could resemble civilization. It took three separate flights, 100 miles each way in a single night, to pull it off. Bar stools and tables were tied to the skids. The bar itself arrived in two sections, suspended on cables.

Although home base was an abandoned plantation northwest of Saigon near the Cambodian border, we ranged up and down the Ho Chi Minh trail and carried out missions in South Vietnam, Cambodia, Laos, and North Vietnam.

The Viet Cong were using Cambodia as a sanctuary and staging area for combat operations against our forces. While our government's policy was not to invade Cambodia, our team operated there with no other impunity than our lives. If caught, we were mercenaries or spies, with no affiliation with the United States. It was incentive enough not to become a prisoner. The Boss and Uncle had been to POW school where the lessons of Korea were simulated.

"It would be a waste of time for you guys," Top told us. "POW status will never be put on your plate if you get caught where we ain't supposed to be. Don't cry, just die. That's the way it is."

Wires asked me, "Would you give me a hypo if we couldn't get out?"

"Tell you what. If it comes to that, I'll shoot us both full of Thorazine and we can tell the Cong to kiss our asses."

"Yeah, but dope wears off. What do we do then?"

"Eat our tongues," I replied.

"You've been around Top too long, you gung-ho bastard."

We both laughed. It was the only way to deal with that kind of reality.

The closest we came to becoming POWs occurred in North Vietnam. It was also the only time that I had to administer the terminal hypo. Our mission was to assassinate a regular North Vietnamese Army colonel who was successfully attacking our forces in the highlands along the border. His tactic was to reinforce a defeated Viet Cong regiment with regular North Vietnamese Army personnel and counterattack in areas presumed secure. Fresh, well-trained regular army units, disguised as revolutionary Viet Cong, overran garrisons and hamlets with virulent ferocity. One of these battles nearly wiped out a Green Beret outfit. Others were hit hard.

When battlefield intelligence revealed that the attackers were North Vietnamese regulars masquerading in black pajamas, our Army brass was furious. When the identity of the enemy field commander was learned, the Green Berets wanted his ass. The order came down from on high.

"Show extreme prejudice. Disregard costs."

The Boss had a prejudicial slant of his own on the operation.

"Somebody gave the Green Berets a bloody nose. Now they're asking Rangers to go kick ass. To take their revenge. If we can pull this off, I swear to God that I am going to steal every green beret out of the Saigon Officers Club and publicly piss on them."

"Mind if we add a few sissy covers from the NCO Club?" Top asked.

"Let's piss on 'em and then put 'em back where we got 'em," Spook volunteered. It was the only time I can remember when Spook earned a genuine laugh from the team.

We waited for an intelligence break for five weeks before we got the operational go. The entry was through Laos with a difficult transit to the target area. The colonel was being set up by an agent in a hamlet used by North Vietnamese for R&R. The lure was locally made rice wine and a bordello that was considered lush by frontline standards. Our contact was to lead the intoxicated colonel down a rural path toward her pleasure hooch. She was supposed to be a beautiful woman who had his confidence. The deal included extracting her after we greased the colonel. Neither Boss nor Top liked that part of the op, but Uncle assured them that it was necessary.

Fixer and Spook were bumped from the mission, and the remaining seven of us mentally reviewed the last will and testaments that the legal officers had forced on us when we joined the unit. I wondered how the Army might report my death to my parents. At the time, I was supposed to be at Fort Monroe in Virginia.

We used absolute stealth to get into position. The entry angle avoided known populated areas around the hamlet. The woman and the colonel appeared right on schedule, and we hit him so hard and so fast that he was dead before he hit the ground.

The woman panicked. Uncle got to her and quickly learned why. The colonel's officers and their women were on the trail behind them. That was not the worst news. An entire regiment of North Vietnamese regulars was bivouacked only a few hundred yards away. They were poised like a semicircle around our position. She could not warn us. She had tried to divert the colonel and his party, but he was insistent. All was lost. We would all die.

Boss made an immediate decision after Uncle had translated. Muscles was ordered to drag the body into the bush and catch up with us as we moved away by the same route we had come. I was ordered to give the woman a tranquilizer and to keep her quiet as we moved along the escape route.

We had been on the move less than fifteen minutes when the fury of hell broke loose behind us. First there was scattered gunfire, and then flares began to appear in the night sky. Nobody had to tell us that the colonel's body had been found. Nobody had to tell us that the hero's regiment was wildly awake and desperately seeking our blood. We were beyond the perimeter sentries, but it would not take long for them to get our direction. We had counted on six hours of escape time before the colonel was missed. What we got was a few minutes. If they closed the circle or pursued us until daylight, we were history.

"We can't escape and evade on the run," the Boss decided. "Let's find a swamp or rice field and get deep. Maybe Diamond Tim can get them off our asses."

There was no time to booby trap our rear, and to sacrifice a few of us in a rear-guard action against two or three thousand elite troops was senseless. We were going to be overrun.

Top and Wires raced ahead and prepared the swampy field Boss had selected for our burial. It was opportune only because Boss and Top were smart enough to recognize its potential on our inbound. We left the trail and entered a thigh-deep ditch used for irrigation. The banks were deep in mud and thick with high grass and reeds. It would provide perfect concealment at night once we dug in, but daylight would reveal the tell-tales of our presence.

"Dig in deep along a line parallel to the ditch," Top ordered.

"Real deep," Boss added.

Boss and Radio dug side by side in the swampy earth.

"Have you got an extra breathing tube for the girl?" Top asked me.

"She can have mine. I'll use an IV tube off the blood bag."

Uncle helped me attempt to put the girl into the mud, but she was not cooperating. I dug while Uncle instructed her in her native language. I gave her another injection of Thorazine.

Boss was attempting to establish radio contact with our cover gunships. Diamond Tim, at the lead of three gunships, was somewhere twenty-five or more miles off into the cold, night sky. He was hovering on station after a difficult instrument flight that helicopter pilots hate. He was over the horizon, beyond sight and sound, loaded for bear in case we needed him. We needed him.

Boss was giving Tim our position. Radio was rigging a strobe light the size of a quarter at the bottom of a long extension tube. When the tube was extended above the mud, among the reeds, the light could be seen only if you stood directly above it, or if you were a thousand feet in the air.

The woman was not responding immediately to the Thorazine, although the second shot pushed the dosage up to 150 mg. She was still hysterical, fighting our attempts to conceal her and make her breathe through the tube. Top reported our problems to Boss and returned to check on our progress.

"We've got to get down, now," he warned. "They're going to be on us in a few minutes. Boss wants to know if you can guarantee that she won't twitch if you dope her."

"She's out of control. If she can't breathe, she is instinctively going to get up," I warned.

Uncle confirmed. "She's not trained for this. She's hysterical."

"Put her down," Top said.

"Down?" I asked.

"Down forever, damn it! And then get yourselves as deep as you can. This is my last check of the line. I'm going deep myself."

Uncle continued to bury her. His hand was already across her mouth. Despite the tranquilizers, the adrenaline of fear made her eyes bulge. She squirmed under our combined weight. I plunged the deadly hypo into her thigh. She was small. The dose was huge. She died in a convulsive jerk before I could remove the needle.

"Dig in," Uncle ordered. "I'll finish her."

I had squirmed my way under a foot of mud and calmed down enough to establish a regular breathing pattern when my body was aware that there was activity around us. It takes great discipline to be buried and breathe through a tube the diameter of your thumb. It is worse when a few hundred fanatics are on top of you. If they found one of us, they would find us all. That's why we had to kill her. Maybe none of us would escape.

Boss stayed up to transmit as long as he could. By that time he could see soldiers silhouetted all around us. It was just a matter of time before we were discovered. His last order was a gutsy one. He told Tim the situation and directed him to unload directly on the strobe.

"On it?" Tim asked.

"Do it! We're deep. They're all over us! Do it now!"

The three gunships located the pulsating strobe, a beacon observable only from their height. They could not see the enemy. The enemy soldiers may have heard the distant rotors, but no infantryman fears a helicopter at night. Then Diamond Tim made his first pass with machine guns and rockets. The Vietnamese were caught in the open by surprise. They died by the score, maybe by the hundreds. After the second pass by all three gunships, Boss raised his head out of the slop and directed another devastating pass at the retreating mob. Top came along the line, and we got up, making a dash away from the covering fire. By the time the gunships had expended all their ordnance, we were out of immediate danger and moving toward our dawn extraction point in Laos. Our cat still had a few more lives.

A couple of weeks later there was a rash of soggy green berets in Saigon service clubs.

Let me attempt to describe a phenomenon that most combat soldiers have experienced. If you put a human being in grisly life-and-death situations for a long period of time, and he survives, he passes a threshold of emotionally based fear and reaches a state of animal instinctiveness beyond the subject-object way humans are socially conditioned. A kind of shock occurs when the mind releases control to the body, to its automatic patterns and habits. A well-trained soldier can perform in this mode. He can endure extreme physical hardships and pain. He can be deadly efficient without his own mortality coming to mind. He is invulnerable to hesitation. He is extremely dangerous.

New soldiers in the field have an enthusiasm and naiveté that fades when they get bloodied. Veterans stare into the distant hills and experience the paradoxical inner peace that organized killing can produce. When you give up the hope of surviving, you are free of fear. When the mind is released from the fear of death, any behavior is possible. The experience is one of numbness. Chaotic events occur in slow motion. You are more an observer than a participant; yet your body reacts to the situations with its highest degree of training.

Although the phenomenon I've described wears off like a drug a few days or weeks after the intensity of combat, it becomes an acquired mind-body mode. In Vietnam, after we were bloodied, the act of planning another mission would provoke its onset. By the time we were en route, our faces were already set into stone, our hearts frozen, our limbs transformed into flexible steel. We lost personality and assumed animal character.

After Vietnam, for the rest of my life, I have never experienced physical fear. In some respects, I died there. Further living carries no threat. You can't kill what has already died. That is not an attitude. It is a trait. Something that has been bred into me by serving as a merchant of death.

Cats

George Uriah

That cat sounds familiar, Joe Duke thought. Yes, cat was the right word for him, Joe decided. The guy was smooth, or at least pretended to be. Something about him suggested he had spent many nights hanging out in alleys and other dives until the sun was just around the corner. Besides, he talked just like a crazy cat Joe knew when he was in the Army; even the tone of his voice was a dead match. The first time Joe heard the new guy speak, he almost turned around and looked for the crazy cat he once knew as Sanchez.

Except that Sanchez was Mexican, or maybe Puerto Rican. Sanchez was half white too, but when you're anything less than all white in America, you're whatever else you are. The math should have been simple, and it baffled Joe that it was not. This new cat was Italian, or so he maintained. His looks suggested the claim was dubious. Joe had not seen too many fair skinned, sandy-haired Italians. Maybe his family was from near the Alps. Or maybe he was just half.

This new cat at work bragged to everyone with whom he spoke about how he came from the cold streets of somewhere in New Jersey. He worshipped the Philadelphia Eagles, a trait he shared with the last cat Joe knew from New Jersey, the guy with the vague Hispanic heritage. According to Sanchez, no one from Philly truly liked the Eagles, not enough to be a real fan. Only people from Jersey were real Eagles fans. The Eagles were Jersey's team, and only theirs, and you couldn't convince him otherwise. Everyone from every corner of PA, as those affiliated with the state called Pennsylvania, was a Steelers fan, or should be. Joe doubted this was true. And forget about mentioning the Jets and Giants actually played in New Jersey; it would be fruitless.

"That makes no sense. Surely someone from Philadelphia likes the Eagles?" Joe had asked.

"Naw." Every Jersey cat he knew spoke in absolute, grandiose claims. Heaven forbid you questioned the beauty or sanctity of the place. It was not even good enough for someone like Joe to concede parts of New Jersey were kinda nice and Cape May was one of the finest seaside towns he had visited. Anyway, it was more fun to see Sanchez's reaction when he referred to the state as a dump. "Ain't no garden that I ever seen in the Garden State," Joe said in the same rigid terms to keep pace.

The only time Sanchez had not strutted his words was the last time Joe had spoken with him.

"Remember our boy Lyndon?" Sanchez asked, dispensing with the usual pleasantries that accompany a phone call to someone with whom you have not talked in more than a year.

"That crazy little red-headed Fighting Irish look-alike from New York?" Joe asked, as if there had been another Lyndon they both had known.

"He's dead."

"What?" Joe didn't know what to say. "How?"

"He was on his second tour in Iraq and his convoy ran over a homemade explosive. Killed him before he could have known what happened."

Why, Joe wondered, though he did not ask the question aloud. He and Lyndon were going to get out of the Army at the same time. Lyndon was going to get a job in security and spend time with his wife and newborn daughter. "She's gonna save me from the Army," Lyndon said of his daughter. But he got scared of having to get a real job and reenlisted, and it was just Joe that got out. After Joe heard Lyndon had died, he scoured the internet for news accounts, and each one stated that he had called his daughter right before the last mission to tell her he loved her. At least she had those words to carry with her throughout the rest of her life, along with all of the sorrows that would come when she was old enough to know.

This new cat talks too much for his own good, Joe thought. The two had been in the same training class at the Cosmodemonic Television Sales Corporation where Joe had started work to make extra money while he was in graduate school, a job that would nearly slash away his soul before he got away from its clutches. The new cat had started work with his kitten, an airhead who would supposedly soon become his wife. "The word dingbat instantly comes to mind," Joe thought the first time he heard her speak, laughing uneasily after each verbalized thought. But maybe she was the brighter of the couple.

For three weeks, Joe heard all about the new cat's troubled life. He had grown up on the streets. He had tried to run with the mob when he could, which apparently was not very often. Evidently the mob didn't like him as much as he liked them. They didn't take to addicts, at least not to the extent that this cat was. The mob could be funny that way. He got mixed up with heroin pretty bad in high school, the new cat claimed, almost bragging. He was far too open about his life, Joe maintained. If it were me, I would conveniently omit that part of my life in tales told to strangers, much less brag about it. There was a lot Joe kept to himself.

Besides, Joe's good friend Morricone from his Army days really was in the mob now. His father had ties and Morricone had faced limited employment opportunities when he left the military, so it seemed like a good idea and a natural fit. But he felt no need to advertise the fact and kept his mouth pretty shut. Of course, if Morricone was a cat, he'd be a big Tsavo cat, something on the Serengeti, a predator just like Sanchez and Lyndon and the rest of the crew. "We was kings back then," Morricone would later reminisce. "We was lions and the whole world was ours." This new guy was just an alley cat.

But then this new cat found his kitten. She straightened him out for good, or so he claimed. He finally loved something more than the heroin. He finally loved someone more than himself. He told a sorrowful story about calling his estranged dad and telling him that he had met someone and cleaned up and was getting married. The cat's father had his doubts, and the two resumed not speaking to one another.

The cat's situation vaguely reminded Joe of his own. He would not have touched heroin, though. To him it was open desperation and there were certain things Joe did not want to admit. But he struggled with alcohol, a legally acceptable but no less lethal drug in Joe's hands. And a woman had sobered Joe up. And Joe had not spoken with his father in years. Joe actually married the girl, and, when he did, he did not bother telling his father. Later that year, Joe sent his father a Christmas card with a picture of the newlyweds, and Joe and his father went right back to not communicating with one another.

The new cat failed to show up for work one day, Joe noticed. The kitten was missing as well. He asked someone where they were. Evidently, the vintage Spiderman lunch box the cat carried like it was a CIA briefcase was full of the drugs he'd been selling. The cops came in and made a scene in the middle of his shift the day before, Joe was told. The cat had fooled everyone. No telling who the cat really was. They, whoever they were, said the cat had only taken the job to sell more drugs in a call center that begged for them. People did it all the time. He was probably turned in by a rival. Funny how alley cats can be territorial like that. Maybe his old man was right after all. Maybe people don't change.

People had been saying these things about Joe for some time too, that no one really knew who he was. These same people also commented that tigers don't lose their stripes. Joe considered that thought as he chugged from his second full Solo cup of Jack and Coke on his way home from work, drinking while driving so his wife didn't catch him in the act. Later she would maintain that he was never present during the marriage. "But I was home every night," he would counter. Joe muttered something to himself about being a wolf in sheep's clothing. Maybe old Dad was right after all.

Every evening before he drove away from work, he mixed his first robust drink of the night, stiff enough to make even an experienced drinker like Joe choke at first. Maybe the only thing he liked in life during those days was the first unspoken promise of a chemical entering his bloodstream and the pledge it would soon find its way to his brain. As he poured, he was mesmerized by the look of cola mixing with liquor. If you looked closely and quickly enough, it was almost like a bit of blood diluting the drugs in a hypodermic before the high is injected.

Joe really did make a sincere effort to sober up when he got married. He tried to think back to when he started drinking. It was when Sanchez told him Lyndon died, but maybe that was just the raindrop that broke the overtaxed dam. One by one the people from that particular past had fallen away. It used to be the lot of them cats, driving drunk in fast cars and looking for brawls and women and screaming fuck the world. Now they were grown up or moved on. But Lyndon was different. Joe had just lost touch with the rest of those cats. He always had the option to look them up again. Not so with Lyndon. Now when he googled him he just got the newspaper articles about his death, how he had just talked to his wife and daughter that same morning.

Joe had asked why. But he wasn't asking about Lyndon. And he wasn't asking about war. It was why any of this? So little of his life made sense, and that had been the case long before Lyndon died. No telling when it began and what caused it. At least he wasn't just an alley cat. And he still had a woman who might save him from himself a second time.

Joe finished off the whiskey and cola in the driveway. He had polished off an alcoholic evening's worth in twenty minutes, tossing the bottle out the window somewhere along the way to hide the evidence. Never before in his life had he purposefully drank enough to black out. Those days, he did it every night because he wanted the world to go away, if only for a few hours. If I drink enough, he would later maintain, I don't have to be me for a while, and I don't have to live this life of mine. He stumbled into the condo, where his wife was already asleep, and wished he had no secrets. There was a lot he'd like to bring up if he knew how.

Patrick Kelly

The Measuring of Light

I.

This story is about me, but it is more about a girl named Clara, whom once I couldn't save. But then I think I did save her, when our Mississippi coastal town was wiped from the map during Hurricane Katrina. When I think of her, a bright blasted moon rises overhead in my memory.

At the saving, it was dark here at first and eruptions like lily pads strayed over black rain water. I clung to her while orange chests pulled us from our homes into a shallow boat, couraged by rough talk, tender hands. I had showed them where to go, thinking: "He has eruptions, angry eruptions like the new world being created here." I prayed He'd erect a statue, pretty, but short and of bright rain. There'd be sizzling, like acid, like celebratory seltzer, and no pain, only an awareness leaking from slumping shoulders as crows clawed my insolence, pecking. I felt silent men pull us from fogged voids, working steady now. See. Rough hands. Tan hands. Burnt crusted crimson hands. Rainbows of light, dark sienna, God's Noah promise. Her limp eyes were vacant like black button eyes on a sogged doll. We moved on cluttered water as I blew into her mouth. No worries, the men said as they nodded to each other. The moon is still there, I thought, but in a shelter, praying to the God who sent these eruptions. This rain. This flood.

II.

I was warned. No, not by anybody who had my best interest at heart, kindly looking out for me when I made this or that mistake. I was warned by the universe, the thing that tickles you behind the ear when you pass a broken church steeple or feel the accusing, darting, hung-down gaze of a limping dog or fight the whip of a hurricane while clinging to a tree limb as your hometown is torn from beneath your still breathing dreams. I should have seen it coming, but I ignored the signs through the breaking years. I plunged into the future like a tattered town crier, howling that all was well, even while shudders swept through me and my eyesight blurred, limbs growing stiff from a cold that blew into my bones like cancerous tissue. My howling was shadowed by my actions, which assured folks that if they tried hard and were positive, if they smiled sweetly, if they treated each other nicely, everything would be alright. I saw a spy for the national service eavesdropping on military radio traffic. I saw an editor talking on the phone, sitting through media events, quietly taking notes—a fly on a wall trying desperately to outpace spiders. Ghosts travel with me. Ghosts act through me. Ghosts become me. Ghosts greet me with a knowing wink and a small bouncy jig. A pirate? An adventurer? A gypsy? A knave? Are you truly happy? Can you take it all in? I hit the refresh button like Odysseus.

There were crusaders to the Holy Land who would kill everyone, letting God sort their souls. I fill each day in activity, killing minutes rolling toward quickening breezes. I try and jig one step ahead of the Devil. We eventually hate what we fear. I mumble and draw in the ground with my toe. But like a Phoenix, hope can also rise from fear, negating the hate; the equation equals and I rub away the mud scrapings on the pavement with my worn shoe. My mercy prevails over my wrath.

III.

Things have changed around here I mumbled this morning as I headed to my car, a sleek red speedster. My vision is clear. When I enter a library, the people have changed. I hardly know how. Sometimes I sneak up on a thought before I see it whole, edging myself through a row of whitewashed sepulchers and peeking around rough-marked stones, finally grabbing, hugging, caressing the trembling jokester, the thought-image, wrestling it to the swollen ground like a biblical Jacob. Something is hiding just beyond surfaces that continues to whisper, even as we try to ignore the rustle. I squint my eyes. Fairies like to hide in the cracks of the world. Scientists have covered over the wonder of it with math and equations that continue to lengthen. They have swept magic from our eyes like so many butterflies flapping, like swooning swans. Clara taught me that. She would remember a Muslim quote: "Those who unjustly eat up the property of orphans, eat up a fire into their own bodies: they will soon be enduring a blazing fire."

I look at skylights overhead with gray light streaming; my glasses fog and darken. The fireflies blink out when I puff. The floor lurches a little under my feet with people I meet, like Clara, who works at the library. I knew her when we were both very young. I check the crowd at the grocery store, look quickly to the pizza place. Do I see her across the street, standing in a stadium? I step from the curb, toward the opposite sidewalk; raised hand, sign of recognition, brushing back of hair, a flair from her blue eyes. Oh my God. Is that. . . ? Some proud ship? My sailing anchor? It's moving much too fast, hits me, and I drown. I open my eyes, try to remember the dream, but it quickly fades. Something about flying toward a planet, a bright star thrown across endless black, then space is rolling over and I'm watching a blue light blow closed, dimming away slowly, as dreams do.

IV.

Listen. Us kids today—we remember the past, we remember the past—sing and play hopscotch on the long-healing pavement. See. Hear. The moon rose overhead tonight. We sing, we hop. But it was dark here then, and pockmarks and eruptions strayed over black water as rain fell. As we hopped, hopped, hopped. We clung to mothers while feral men pulled us through moist, warm chambers; but now it's only through bedroom windows into boats, always couraged by tender hands. The surf crashes into mist. The surf crashes into mist. The mist is cold and scalding in the crash. The mist is cold and scalding in the crash. We sing and dance in a mist that fogs our past, ourselves, our fathers and grandfathers, and kneel under broken branches. We no longer lead armies with flags unfurled but are bent by kingdoms we could not build. Erect me into a statue, we now sing. Not pretty, but short and made of red gumdrops melting in rain. There is sizzling like bubbling seltzer. There is no pain. Only awareness leaking from slumping shoulders. The gulls claw and peck our eyes. Peck our eyes, peck our eyes. Before flapping, we sing after another tomorrow we never saw, never saw. Like another ocean. Like sunbaked deserts whose God folded eight black sockets into pale sandy faces before turning away. The radio in my head again: *Longer boats are coming to win us. They're coming to win us. They're coming to win us. Longer boats are coming to win us.* The moon has eruptions too, hiding them like a young girl. Red, angry eruptions from when the world was being created, like womanhood, in our past, our past, like the new world being created here. The rough, silent men pulled a mother and girl from the fogged void then, working steady now but worried. We sing while white silvery lights stab down to us. See. Rough hands. Red hands. Brown hands. Burnt, dark sienna hands. A rainbow of light; God's Noah promise. The limp mother's eyes were vacant like black button eyes of a girl's doll. The surf crashes into mist. The surf crashes into mist. The mist is cold and scalding in the crash. The mist is cold and scalding in the crash. We still hear it howling at the edge of some scarred and sacred town. We moved off through steamy, cluttered water, and the moon was still there—we sing. Silent. Ashamed. Like the others who will gather, praying to a God who sends these eruptions. This rain, this flood. This hope that was washed away from our singing and dance.

I look up from my bedside and it's early morning. I remember it's Saturday, and mean to go to the library to see Clara, who used to be my sweetheart in high school. Now we're just good friends. Something is reminding my head with sharp quick blows. Six months ago I rented this house. I make money selling freelance articles to the local newspaper. I used to write about politics and people but now write about business and employment trends within an economy ravaged along a bleak, shuttered coastline. I also take pictures of sunsets and sunrises. These are for myself and one other. Rain comes down and thunder rumbles, but it will not throw me. I once thought storms were a sign of bad news but try to ignore them now. It is why I can believe in God and be superstitious too. I've tried to moderate my pagan tendencies through the years. Clara has had a hand in this too, I fear. I can't stop bad news from happening no matter how hard I try, and sunshine always comes out in the end. I have a yearning today, for the cool, musty shelves of the library—where Clara works picking out the books for the town to read—so I decide to go to the library, keeping a weather eye out. I shave and look at myself in the mirror: brown hair cut close, a speck of early gray at the temples—gray, I'm going gray, my roof frays, I must delay, maybe a sunset brown—wire-framed glasses, the face grown a bit plumper and creased over the years, sun-browned in a healthy sort of way. He's—I'm—older than I'd like to be. He sometimes looks in the mirror and doesn't recognize the face staring back, staring back, going back more than he sees, squinting, borrowing quietly from him. It doesn't unnerve him too much anymore. He used to think it meant he was going mad, but now he realizes it only means he's grown older, seen some stuff. Ha! You can't get me there, you ol' Devil, he mumbles and smiles at the mirror. Go sit on your tack! He pat, pat, pats his face smoothed over with razors. He prays that God removes his holy choosing. As for that face, it seems tormented with an everlasting itch for things remote. I love to sail forbidden seas and land on barbarous coasts. When I find himself becoming too pale, I usually sit outside with my face turned toward the sun. Soaking up vitamins, I tell myself from hollowed eyes. Vanity, all is vanity, someone once said. I get dressed after eating breakfast and calling my sister, who lives in California, growing babies, prettily tanned.

V.

After getting into my car I drive to the downtown area, pulling into the library parking lot, and notice a former friend standing outside near the front entrance. I knew the man in high school and have run into him a couple of times; the man is always alone and often downtown, though I am not sure what the man does. I stand looking at the library and the man becomes uncomfortable, unable to understand what is happening. I turn my back to the building and the man relaxes, anxiety visibly draining from his limbs. The man says he is an independent contractor, which usually means he does odd jobs for homeowners and is unemployed. Today the man refuses to answer my hello. The man is bearded with mussed brown hair tied into a short ponytail in back, and always looks a bit tattered around the edges, with worn sleeve cuffs, old gray sneakers. I've always liked him, or at least my memories of him. We were once buddies. Old buddies stored like dusty loafers. I was thinking to myself the years of separation are a mystery that can never be solved. We remember how we once were and cling to long past images, but I think the man has gone a bit crazy, and memories of those times only flicker on and off in the man's eyes. Sometimes the man acts like he is seeing me for the first time. "Hey," I say, as I make my way to the front entrance of the library, giving the man a nod, not sure if we might have a talk. The man is looking from side to side, as if waiting for someone to hide behind his closed door. There is profound meaning in trying to glimpse another person's inner light.

The library's red brick façade casts rippling images in lingering pools of rainwater from the morning's storm. The rain has stopped but the sky is a dark slate, and the parking pavement is slick and black, as black as the screen behind the man's eyes. The air smells clean. I catch a nuance of sea salt as if the water had pulled itself closer to hug the blasted Mississippi coastline.

The man and I were boys during a fish derby years ago. At the time, some haggard fishermen appeared on a local show to talk about a strange craft landing near the river where the navy builds gray war vessels. There were rumors that have never been explained, that the river folk detected mysterious ships. The sheriff's office opened its own investigation. One of the fishermen ended up loony and died in an asylum. We still often hear him whooping. A sad soul will kill you quicker than a bad man, he still whoops with the wind, quoting the lettuce picker. "You just get into town?" the man asks, so I stop to talk, wondering again if the man has mental or just memory problems. I never really left, just moved to another part of town after Hurricane Katrina hit. I'm doing a little work for the newspaper the man holds in his hand, I indicate with my head. We threw newspapers on driveways from our bicycles when young, a long arc of a throw, gliding, then plopping, then sideways skidding.

"Newspapers! Huh!" The man spits on the pavement and glares. "Never get the truth there. I'll give you a story. You write about that." I look at the man and study his eyes, which seem a little bloodshot as if he had already been drinking this morning. They slowly clear for a moment and the glare softens. We're friends again for a second, as if in a soft-lit church, rainbows lighting stained-glass windows and throwing determined shafts over dark pews. Reality is just light measured, Einstein once said in calculations that vexed him the rest of his life.

"You watch yourself now," the man says. "Folks change. I've seen it. Just got back in town, huh? My, my. I heard about it. Heard about you being back. People talk you know. But hey I gotta go. You remember what I told you. Gotta go, now. Going now. Gotta go, now." The man doesn't move but again starts shifting his eyes from side to side as if watching for a bus to arrive, shuffling feet on wet pavement. I imagine the man's waiting for the bar down the street to open, silent smoky figures gathering in the dark. I make a move to go into the library, but the man startles me by grabbing my shoulder and searching my face with his etching eyes. The man's eyes clear for a moment and he speaks in a voice as steady-strong as when the boy barked orders as team captain on the basketball court. A radio from somewhere begins again, but it's only the local preacher on the Gospel hour: *Oh, dear father, can you see me now. Can you see this, myself, you; our chests sorrowfully heaving.*

"You come see me," the man then says with an anxious, earnest intensity. But then, "My my, hey hey, gotta go, gotta go. You come see me now." And then. And then the man's shuffling his feet again with eyes glazed over. He turns his face away, swaying. The man again fades away.

VI.

Finally inside the library, I grab my grandfather's old fishing book and try to sneak out the side door, hoping the man isn't standing there waiting on the street. Clara is with another patron, and I wave. I peek, don't see the man, start walking toward the street away from my car, thinking I'll walk downtown. The shops are now opening like pink orphaned petals.

As I step off the curb I check the sky, which seems to be clearing, and feel a few bright rays of sunshine on my wide, burnt-blue Neptune nose. Some people have called it crusted from parrot clawings.

The visit to the library has set myself musing. *I begin musing about things that hurt my head.* Dying is not what you think. Time doesn't stop. Time doesn't exist. I don't know how long I've been here. Forever? Now? *I am still musing.* When you die, every moment of your life spreads around you in an endless sphere, a bubble of transparent crystal, flowing backward and forward as you observe and try to understand what life meant. *My musings have startled me; will not stop.* Sometimes I think it's the damn books Clara keeps lending me. Before you die you question the meaning of life. At death, your life now questions you. It will never end. It ends, forever ends. The view, the permutations are forever expanding. *The musings hammer my brain.* Like now at the library I saw Clara behind the smooth checkout counter. We were once high school sweethearts. I didn't know whether to hide or boldly approach, and I stumbled a little and swung my face from side to side like a cornered jungle elephant brokering a fierce tiger deal. For a moment I thought I squeaked softly. But my mouth was closed. Whew, I thought. It's only in my head. I checked to see if my tie was straight before remembering that I only wear ties during interviews for newspaper stories. At that moment, looking at her, I remembered a trip we had once taken to the islands, which are located a few miles offshore in my memory's tuning-fork sounds. I think the memory came to me because the air smelled salty that morning from the humidity. Because a gray sky was filtering feeble rays through the large cross-slanted windows, I asked her if she wanted to walk down to the beach pier after work. She said yes, because we still love each other, though that has changed over the years into something created by her outside my understanding, like the meaning of all matter we see, have ever seen, will ever see. All those years before we had walked into the water, until the bitter stinging salt hit us waist high, and I stopped to feel something grow in my heart. I threw my head back, raising my arms toward a sun nestled high in a soft blueing sky. I felt my soul burst from my chest like a divine song, a blossoming flower, then leap into heaven with a reverberating shout, an affirmation, as a small school of flying fish broke through the skin of fluid in a spray of pungent wetness, flashing around Clara like princess jewels. We are programmed to receive and I don't have all the answers. *My musings can't sustain my pulsing brain.*

Nowadays, Clara has me reading too many books, I think. I feel something new is being created and think all our views are joining and changing, becoming one reality, a world without end. When we die, our life's moments will all drift in endless seas of light. The part they play depends on our mental architecture, on whether we've designed a neatly trimmed southern garden, watered, nourished by sprinklers. Open to visitors. Or crumbling castles constructed of tarnished silver clinging to battered moonlit cliffs—Villa La Rondinaia—overlooking stippled, endless sapphire seas. *My musings are hurting my head.* Is there something holding the universe together, a will and imagination blossoming with delight, or is it us and the spaces between? We look around and everything is still a mystery. A place of surprise, joy. And always the fierce roar of the beast is ripping the dark. The beast haunts my dreams. People see pinched and crab-like symbols on shadowy cellar walls, like Plato hearing static of a half-dead radio hissing the dark. I see cracks in the windows of the world and blink, stunned, as light pours in to drown me, sustain me, engulf me, baffle me, muffle the beast's roar. We try holding onto faith, though sometimes it seems a million miles away, like flickering stars. As I have done countless times before, I again step off the library curb and am suddenly bathed in a bright birthing light that comes on quickly, comes often, and which I can never avoid.

VII.

When I was young, I remember picking up chewing gum from the street pavement and placing it in my mouth, the grit melding with the fleeing flavor, and mashing it softly with my teeth, a test of will and desire. Clara and I have always lived here, and the gum never seems to change, though somehow now, ever since Hurricane Katrina, it tastes saltier. When I was younger, other children would laugh and make peeing jokes if my prize was yellow. Often it was a dull red, or more often gray, but I still remember sucking the flavor while swallowing the grit, a philosophy that still sustains me. Clara would just say I was weird. Look down, look down, the Devil would bray, and I will feed you if hearts are brave. Look up, look up, angels would sing to me in crystal verse, and I would think of Clara, this neighbor girl my age, Clara, about five years old, and how we would steal toast from our breakfast tables, meet in the garage to feed each other, pull off our shorts for show-and-tell. I once fell from my parents' white roof, the one with wood paneling, and cracked my head while she was in the car eating burnt toast. She screamed. Some people came running. I was punished for three days in my room with nothing but burnt wheat toast to eat. Often, we would steal off to a nearby canyon and sit near the edge looking down at the far bottom, green thorns, sharp rocks showing the way. She tumbled one day, rolling to the bottom while my heart stopped beating because I was too small to follow. Her father swept in and slid down after, picking her up and clawing back, blood on her face and his arms, while she swore at him in small child curses, like pigeon coos slapping his ears. I remember her socks were a pale pink. His shirt was red with a small logo.

My father once built a playset in the backyard with chain swings and chinning bars for kids to scrabble on, while mother listened to rock-n-roll on a small wireless in the house, the thin, tinny sound floating over green grass and disappearing into cobalt skies. He missed a washer though once, dropped it, and we all walked around feeling with our bare feet until it wriggled itself under my squirmy toes like a lead worm, and I was a hero.

After work, Clara and I reach the beach and walk toward the end of the long pier. I look back briefly and seem to see my two dead uncles, gray and ragged like gentle old fishermen, but laughing and looking at each other with friendly feelings, like two dirty, delicious dogs taking a noble walk, with 70s rock music playing in the background and 8,000 fish splashing to the beat. They died during Hurricane Katrina, a storm whose marks still wound this small town. The pier wood is clammy this evening from the earlier rain, but the air smells clear as glass, and stars are rising. At the pier's end, I climb down into my little boat's cabin and retrieve a memory on which to dream. I pull out my logbook and lick the end of a long pencil. I'm a compulsive note-taker. Clara says it's cute. It worries me a little. I note that dreams are simple but subtle, layered and feathered into a geological strata of time. Like pebbles, we pluck them gently from the thin, yellow shoreline and place them slowly into a scruffy leather pouch, like tonight with Clara and the light breeze moving her hair. I want to remember it. At such times I hold the memories close, almost lovingly, roll them smoothly with my warm breath, toss them into wet waves of nearby breathings, which halt suddenly in time. There is endless life in these dreams, countless hues on this journey, much struggle, an abundance of solving, but I will not decipher or decode because a church father once visited me and soured all the parish pies.

I remember one dream. A small deck is dimly lit. Two benches sit on either side of the space, which could be a carved, rocky cave or a throbbing human cell. Is it a distant yellow orb swollen with angel wings, first glimpsed by that grizzled Italian schemer? The walls waver with a dull gray light spreading over swollen timbers, hammered into place. Crude, unknowable pictures pierce the walls. Seawater, smelling of salty urine, pools from broken iron chains. Thin, tattered yellow vapor squeezes from an undisclosed ceiling that throbs a musky orange glow. I think I hear a prisoner sighing, but it's Clara calling, and now I have climbed back onto the pier, and Clara clutches my arm tightly.

I think of a house perched on hills that change when I gaze, changing before my will to look, because its light takes time to cross a threshold, not true to itself but impermanent; in a tree branch, on a sun-dappled street, near water. I dare not climb stairs into attics because of fears that strike cold. I can show you fear in toes paralyzed from dusty cloth, broken toys, old machines, smoky mirrored dreams. Sometimes I chop a path toward it, hurl myself down dirt roads, through clammy forests, clicking whistling swamps, snowy frozen peaks, dotted with bent sorrowful statues. I stagger to the cluttered edge of a great metropolis, smothered with muffled voices, staining the night air. Are there faces in the windows? A voice sternly whispers and then disappears. I hear the sound of moments passively stretching away. There is profound meaning in our sense of loss, our inadequacy to express it. A church father once visited me, but his deafness stopped the chickens from laying and set the forest beast pacing and sniffing our dreams.

VIII.

A light wind is now beating, worrying the glowing currents of my memories' passions, roiling their yaw and pitch. Clara clutches my arm tighter, but she is smiling, wild and free. Soon, a murmuration of starlings with flaming torches carries me forward on its swooping, heaving shoulders. I sit still, paralyzed from their unearthly singing, gazing toward a smoking mountain flecked with distant water. My canvas sea bag of worn books lies spilled behind the starlings' flight, my staggered path. There is profound meaning in our wish to endure in the face of endless time; Clara saved me with this.

"Remember that story I wrote you about stars? For your birthday?" Clara suddenly looks over to me in my fussing about. "I always remember it at night when I'm looking at the stars. See that big one?" She points. She starts reciting, her face softly glowing. "I move toward a burning distant star," she begins, pointing upward, and I gaze out over the waves tipped with moonlight. "It lights the beginning," she continues softly. "It lights the ending. It pierces the cold, dark nothing of never knowing. It lights the everything of forevertime. It began as itself. It ends as itself. It burns with ripples forever expanding. It shines forever. And ever. And evermore." She looks at me a little slyly. "Do you remember the last line?" "Yes," I say. "I close my bending eyes with hope," she finishes softly, eyes closed.

"Pat?" she asks. "Yes," I answer, listening to the salty waves, lightly slapping the pier pilings. "Oh Pat! Aren't things just the best?" She says it with the quiet conviction of confirming creation. To her, we two remain the primal electrons swirling shakily around a shimmering nucleus I cannot see but hold firmly in my mind.

I look at her short brown hair, poking from underneath her backward baseball cap, feel her arm on mine, notice her eyes slowly blinking, and then shining outward like the burning beacon of a neutron star. I touch her cheek with my fingertips, and she bends her cheek toward my hand. "Yes," I say quietly. "It is wonderful to think so, isn't it."

We live in a dream. We are encouraged by light. We avoid the dark. We are pursued by the past, as the past has pursued Clara and myself. If we can just make one more step, draw one more breath, shade our eyes one more time, we will see it, know it, feel it, somehow touch its brightness, before we are beat back by the crest and backward tide of time's inevitable sorrows.

Cindy McDermott
I Wonder How She's Doing and My Connections

1. I Wonder How She's Doing

We sit in her small kitchen in a small farmhouse in small-town U.S.A. Two daughters play ring-around-the-rosy in the adjoining living room, too young to understand. CACO, the Navy's Casualty Assistance Calls Officer, speaks to my widow. He reviews details on how her husband's body will arrive. She receives the specifics. So courteous, so polite, so numb.

The phone rings. Probably another neighbor wanting details. A family friend, a Vietnam vet, leaves the table to answer. News travels fast in a small town. Friends and family would soon arrive, bringing tuna noodle casseroles and homemade pies, giving a different meaning to the words "comfort food." Busybodies phone the media, alerting reporters, who call me for verification.

"I can't confirm anything. DoD guidelines specify 48 hours to notify primary and secondary next of kin. Watch the website." There's nothing to hide. Just nothing I can say. Everybody knows he's dead, but the computer hasn't made it official.

After hours of discussions, my widow's clipped answers tell me she's overloaded with details and grief. CACO promises to return the next day. We depart, followed by the Vietnam vet.

"How was he killed?" he asks.

CACO exhales. "His Humvee rolled over an IED."

"At least he didn't burn to—" His mouth begins to tremble. His gaze averts to the cornfield across the road.

CACO fills the silence. "I want you to know he volunteered for the convoy."

The vet lasers a stare; he knows the truth. CACO and I pass guilty looks. We've just fed him a standard message the military uses when no other words bring comfort.

But what could my CACO say?

"He knew what he was doing"?

"In defense of his country"?

"He died a hero"?

What military member goes into battle longing for death, to become a hero? That only happens in movies, glamorizing war and boasting of patriotism. Packed with sugary words glorifying love of country, the flag, and apple pie in an attempt to cover its horrific bitterness.

The goal is to come back. Not in a box. Not with pieces missing. Not with nightmares that blast you awake with your own screams. Not with guilt so heavy relief comes by eating your gun.

The truth is, you never come back the same.

*

I shake my head and exhale. I'm in the present, in front of my bathroom mirror, brushing my teeth. Yet another time I've lost myself. When memories of nearly 15 years ago slip into my simple tasks. No trigger. No control.

I've lost touch with my CACO and my widow. I wonder how she's doing. Then again, the outcomes might be too much for both of us. Wounds that shouldn't be opened. Mine so insignificant when compared to hers.

Water runs over the bristles, rinsing out the leftover toothpaste. I tap the brush on the sink to remove the excess. The drops meld together, forming an escape route to the drain. If only they would carry my haunting memories with them.

2. My Connections

Sharing guarded details impacts my soul more than imagined. A part of the healing process, they say. Now, I'm not so sure.

The lobby offers a respite from the hot glare of the lights and invading eyes. I angle my forehead against the window, cooled by the winter air, to quell the throbbing.

A timid voice guides me back to the present. "Could I talk about what you just read?"

I draw a deep breath, unsure of the response I'll reap. Will I be accused of not loving my country because I question his death? Will I be berated for not questioning it enough? I turn to receive my review and encounter Opal.

Lines of hard memories etch her face, yet they frame caring eyes and a concerned smile. We connect through a warm handshake. My left hand folds over our kindred grip.

She had positioned herself in the back row during an afternoon of veterans sharing stories about military experiences. As I read my piece, a magnet of unknown influences pulled my gaze to her again and again. Perhaps a dark, emotional camaraderie linked us. A tissue, never far from her eyes, attempted to capture tears before they escaped down her face.

"I cried the entire time you read your piece. I had a CACO when my son was killed."

She shares details of her experience. The willingness to go above and beyond, by the CACO team, and yet the miscommunications because no handbook exists to deal with the death war brings. No step-by-step manual like the military usually demands. She tells me the Marine CACOs she has had over the years brought her consolation. She maintains contact with some.

"Promise me you'll reach out to your widow. It will bring her comfort to know you still care, and you need that connection too."

My head nods in agreement, but I'm unsure of the direction to take. The only certainty is my soul has been touched again by the death of a military brother.

*

I talk with my family and friends. I talk with my fellow vets. I talk with my god. Finally, I talk with me.

One night I'm moved to reach for my phone. A pull, a tug. Something signals me to begin. I track down my CACO on Facebook.

I send a few lines.

Do you remember her?
What about her children?
I wonder how's she's doing?

In less than a minute I have a reply. He has remained close to her all of these years.

"Why do you ask?" he writes.

I break my story into short pieces. The grief, the guilt, the wondering. He offers to speak by phone. Over the next hour, we talk about our lives and Sally.

Her girls, playing ring-around-the-rosy, remain fixed in my mind. But they've graduated college, are starting lives of their own. Sally's moved to Colorado, her home state. So has my CACO. They live in different cities but close. Wasn't planned that way. Just happened.

He recalls escorting her to the Social Security Office to pick up Joe's death benefit. Two hundred dollars. So disheartening; hardly worth the trip, he adds.

Military funds don't cover the entire cost of the funeral. The church and community step in to make up the difference. "Unforgivable to have a military widow write a check to bury her sailor," he says. "But there's nothing forgiving about war."

CACO shares his own struggles. Volunteered for multiple, back-to-back deployments across the world. Years away to escape the memories. It's a plan so many of us employ. If we don't have time to consider the past, it won't haunt us. It's a strategy, but one that never works.

He tells me the ten-year mark of Joe's death hit especially hard for Sally. The anniversary of an adoration that didn't endure. A remembrance bringing sorrow. But with friends and family, she pulled through.

Now, in less than a month, she would remarry. CACO and his wife are attending. Her veil of sadness is lifting; one of love is sweetly cascading into place. She's moving on to a new life, offering the hope of the same meaningful affection she lost so many years ago.

He proposes to put us in touch but after the wedding. "No need to dredge up those memories during such a joyous time. She's writing a new chapter. Let's not help her turn back to one that brought such sadness and pain. Not now."

I agree. In fact, do I need to speak with her at all? She's happy. The children are well. My questions are answered. Nearly 15 years of her life summed in a phone conversation.

A smile inches across my face. I consider how this story has come together thanks to a stranger touched by my writing. Her strength and concern encouraged me to connect the disjointed lines of my narrative. CACO and I bond over our accounts of working through death. It's a storyline filled with grief and even guilt because we remain among the living. And then there's Sally. She'll always be my widow, but I'll no longer worry about how things turned out for her. Joe's death will forever be a part of her history, of my history. But now, I'll wonder how she's doing with a new love. A pleasant path to wander for the rest of her life.

It's an opportunity for each of us to turn a page. My military mind says the t's are crossed and the i's are dotted, time to move on. But my uneasy soul signals the mission isn't complete.

"CACO, when the time is right, would you tell her I called?"

Contributor Bios

Sheri McQuiston Anderson is the wife of an Air Force veteran who served in Afghanistan and Iraq. Sheri is a Southerner by birth, but after many military moves, she and her family now call Colorado home. She holds a BA in English and an MA in English Rhetoric and Composition, and is a researcher of student veterans' issues. She loves the ocean, dark chocolate, World War II history, and a good game of Scrabble.

Jason Arment served in OIF as a Machine-Gunner in the USMC. He's earned an MFA in CNF from VCFA. His work has appeared in *The Iowa Review*, the 2017 *Best American Essays*, *The New York Times*, among other publications, and on ESPN. His memoir, *Musalaheen*, stands in stark contrast with other narratives about Iraq, in both content and quality. Jason lives in Denver, where he coordinates the Denver Veterans Writing Workshop with Lighthouse. Much of his work can be found at jasonarment.com.

Rachael Attanasio is an actor and artist living in the greater NYC area. The photograph was taken at her cousin's combat medic graduation ceremony at the Joint Base in San Antonio, Texas, during their final march back to their barracks.

Christopher Baumer is a veteran of wars and white waters. You can find him somewhere in southern Oregon, wandering the banks of the Rogue River, lost among the trees. He holds an MFA from Oregon State University, and his work can be found in *Atticus Review*, *Unbroken Journal*, *As You Were: The Military Review*, and *0-Dark-Thirty*.

Randy Brown embedded with his former Iowa Army National Guard unit as a civilian journalist in Afghanistan, May–June 2011. A 20-year veteran with a previous overseas deployment, he subsequently authored the poetry collection *Welcome to FOB Haiku: War Poems from Inside the Wire* (Middle West Press, 2015). His poetry and non-fiction have appeared widely in literary print and online publications, including *Stone Canoe*, *Drunken Boat*, *F(r)iction*, and *So It Goes: The Literary Journal of the Kurt Vonnegut Museum and Library*. As "Charlie Sherpa," he blogs about citizen-soldier culture at www.redbullrising.com, and about military-themed writing at www.aimingcircle.com.

Eric Chandler is the author of *Hugging This Rock: Poems of Earth & Sky, Love & War* (Middle West Press, 2017). He's a US Air Force veteran (active duty and Minnesota Air National Guard). He flew 145 combat missions and over 3000 hours in the F-16. He's a member of Lake Superior Writers and the Military Writers Guild. Eric is a husband and father who cross-country skis as fast as he can in Duluth, Minnesota.

Amie Charney is a poet and fiction writer living in San Antonio, Texas. She has an MFA in Fiction from the University of California–Riverside, and begins teaching this fall at San Antonio College. Amie is a proud Marine Corps wife and has thrived through seven combat tours in support of her husband Michael and children, Lauren and Alex.

Sarah Colby is the wife of an active-duty Army Chaplain currently stationed at Fort Sam Houston, Texas, and mother to a son in the Navy. She is intimately familiar with military life and writes to be a voice for the mostly untold stories of families and loved ones during these years of protracted conflict. Sarah is currently working on a manuscript of poems about her military experiences.

J. F. Connolly is a retired Lieutenant Colonel, USAR. He has published 100+ poems. His latest work is *Picking Up the Bodies*.

Jocelyn Corbin is a U.S. Army veteran and teacher. She has taught high school English Language Arts and Reading in Kentucky since 2010. She is married to an active-duty Army officer and has four children. Her writing has been featured in the books *Beyond the Uniform, Confessions of a Military Wife*, and *D is for Deployment*.

Scott Ennis served in the U.S. Army (Active Duty, Reserves, and National Guard) from 1983–1996. Service provided him the opportunity to attend college, earning a BA in English. Upon realizing that his name contained the word "sonnet," Scott became a sonneteer. His sonnets are often inspired by his military service.

Christopher Farris is pursuing his second Bachelor's degree at the University of Arkansas in preparation for a working retirement. He has spent his life in either the military (enlisted in the United States Air Force and was an officer in the Arkansas Army National Guard) or in the halls of corporations.

Robert Morgan Fisher grew up a military dependent. His father was a career Naval Flight Officer. His fiction and essays have appeared *in Teach. Write.*, *The Wild Word*, *The Arkansas Review*, *Red Wheelbarrow*, *The Missouri Review Soundbooth Podcast*, *Dime Show Review*, *0-Dark-Thirty*, *The Seattle Review*, and many other publications. He has a story in the 2016 Skyhorse Books definitive anthology on speculative war fiction, *Deserts of Fire*, and in the 2018 Winterwolf Press *Howl of the Wild* anthology. He's written for TV, radio, and film. Robert holds an MFA in Creative Writing from Antioch University–Los Angeles, and is currently on the teaching faculty of Antioch University–Santa Barbara. Since 2016, Robert has led an acclaimed twice-weekly writing workshop for veterans with PTSD in conjunction with UCLA.

Garlen Wayne Funnell spent one tour in Vietnam, 1966–67, at Chu Lai. He was Aviation Ordnance man [AO] [6511]/[0311] attached to 1st MAW – MAG-13. He was in Operation Rolling Thunder. He did USMC boot camp in 1965 with platoon 247 at MCRD at San Diego. After his service, he went to Purdue University. He graduated in 1973 with a BS in Electronic Technology. He became an IRCM expert and traveled the Middle East and Europe between 1983 and 1987.

Bill Glose is a former paratrooper and combat veteran with the 82nd Airborne Division. The author of four poetry collections, Glose has been published in *The Missouri Review*, *Rattle*, *The Sun*, and *Narrative Magazine*, among others. In 2011, he was named the *Daily Press* Poet Laureate and in 2017 he was featured by NPR on *The Writer's Almanac*.

Jessica M Granger holds an MFA from the University of Texas–El Paso. She is an Army veteran, serving from 2001–2010. Her work can be found in *TheNewVerse.News*, *Fredericksburg Literary and Art Review*, *Molotov Cocktail Magazine*, and *As You Were*, among others.

After eight years of active duty in the Air Force (including combat in Vietnam), then six years in the Missouri Air National Guard as a Captain, **Jay Harden** completed a career in the Defense Department, then became a photographer and writer of short stories, poems, and lyrics about love, war, childhood, and personal growth. He is the great grandson of William Harmon Harden, who served as a Sergeant in the 63rd Georgia Volunteer Infantry, C.S.A.

Elise Hempel's poetry has appeared in numerous places over the years, including *Poetry, The Midwest Quarterly, Southern Poetry Review*, and Ted Kooser's *American Life in Poetry*. Able Muse Press published her first full-length collection of poems, *Second Rain*, in 2016. Her father, now 90, is a Korean War veteran.

Gail Hosking grew up as an army brat with a life-long soldier who fought three wars and was eventually killed in Viet Nam. Later, that soldier was awarded a posthumous Medal of Honor. She is the author of the memoir *Snake's Daughter: The Roads In and Out of War* (University of Iowa Press) and the poetry chapbook *The Tug* (Finishing Line Press). Her essays and poetry have been published in such places as *The Fourth Genre, Nimrod International, The Florida Review, The South Dakota Review, Cream City Review, Passages North, Post Road*, and *The Chattahoochee Review*. Several have been anthologized.

Charles Jacobson grew up in Minneapolis, MN, and resided there until he put up his motorcycle and entered the army to avoid incarceration. After basic in Ft. Leonard Wood, MO, he served in noncombat capacity in Chinon, France, in 1962–63, and Alexandria, VA, in 1963–64. Following an honorable discharge, he returned home and studied both the Indochina War and the Vietnam War, and made friends and interviewed vets returning from the war. He is working on a book based on the in-country combat experience of one of those vets during the years 1969–70.

T. S. Johnson was raised by a lower-class family in a small East Texas town. Johnson graduated from the University of Texas–Austin with baccalaureates in journalism and film, working in broadcast news. He later enlisted in the United States Army to pay off his education, and mostly achieved this goal. He married his wife while overseas and left the Army as a commissioned officer. They live in San Antonio, Texas, with their dog, Finch.

Monty Joynes has had 3 previous stories and 3 poems published in *Proud to Be*. His award-winning story, "First Day at An Khe," appeared in Volume 1. Joynes is the librettist of a classical music oratorio, *The Awakening of Humanity*. He is the author of 22 books and continues to publish fiction, poetry, and non-fiction from his mountain home in North Carolina. Joynes served in the Army (1964–1966) with the 91st Evacuation Hospital.

Patrick Kelly was a Russian linquist in the U.S. Army for a number of years, and then spent several years as a newspaper writer and editor. He received a BA in Journalism from the University of Southern Mississippi. He survived Hurricane Katrina by clinging to a tree branch while his home and town were washed away beneath him—and then he wrote about it afterward in a story for the Associated Press. His grandfather was the sailor that John F. Kennedy saved when PT-109 was torn in two by a Japanese destroyer during WWII.

Ben Kingsley is best known for his Academy Award winning role as Mahatma Gandhi. A touch less famous, Affrilachian author **Benjamín Naka-Hasebe Kingsley** has not acted since his third-grade debut as the undertaker in *Music Man*. A Kundiman alum, Ben is currently the 22nd Tickner Writing Fellow and recipient of a Provincetown Fine Arts Work Center fellowship. He belongs to the Onondaga Nation of Indigenous Americans in New York. Peep his recent work in *FIELD, The Georgia Review, jubilat, Kenyon Review, Missouri Review, New England Review, Oxford American*, & *Tin House*, among others.

Cindy McDermott has nearly 21 years of service with the United States Navy as a Public Affairs Officer, retiring as a Commander (O-5) in 2006, as the Public Affairs Department Head, Midwest Readiness Command, Naval Station Great Lakes. For nearly five years, Cindy's been part of a team in Kansas City, Missouri, organizing free writing workshops for vets and their family members using writing as one tool on their pathway of recovery.

Born and raised in Wichita, Kansas, **Lindsey J. Medina** graduated from Kansas State University with a Bachelor's Degree in English and Creative Writing, and simultaneously earned a commission as an officer in the U.S. Air Force. Currently, she is stationed in Japan. Her grandfather served in the Army, her uncle served in the Marine Corps, and her father, aunt, and three of her cousins served in the Air Force.

Kristine Otero served in the U.S. army on active duty from 2003–2007, completing two combat tours in Iraq. She completed two years in the Texas Army National Guard, before being honorably discharged in 2010. She has been published in *0-Dark-Thirty* and through the Colorado Humanities in the anthology *Still Coming Home*. Kristine lives in Denver, Colorado, where she is an active participant in the Denver Veterans Writing Group.

Joseph S. Pete is an infantry veteran of Operation Iraqi Freedom III, an award-winning journalist, a book reviewer, and a frequent guest on Lakeshore Public Radio. He is the author of the forthcoming *Lost Hammond* and *Rust Belt Cantos* books. His writing has appeared in many publications, including *Veterans of Foreign Wars Magazine*, *As You Were*, *Line of Advance*, *0-Dark-Thirty*, and *Dogzplot*. He's not perfect by any stretch but he tries his best.

Gavin Pringle was stationed in Guam aboard the *Chicago*. He was a Petty Officer Second Class during his time there. He was also stationed in Charleston, SC, and Ballston Spa, NY.

Bree Pye is a former U.S. Army photojournalist who is currently working on completing her MFA in creative writing at the University of Colorado at Boulder, where she serves as the Nonfiction Editor for *Timber* journal. Her work has been published in the *Barely South Review*, Southeast Missouri State University Press, and *The Journal of Compressed Creative Arts*.

James Hugo Rifenbark entered the Army late February '70 and worked as a still photographer. He's been married for 40 years to a wonder woman, with whom he shares a love of photography and art.

Billie Holladay Skelley received her bachelor's and master's degrees from the University of Wisconsin–Madison. Her writing has appeared in various journals, magazines, and anthologies in print and online. An award-winning author, she also has written books for children and teens. Her father, Captain Howard Kelly Holladay, served in the Army Air Forces as a B-24 pilot during WWII, and received the Distinguished Flying Cross and the Air Medal with three Oak Leaf Clusters.

Wes Smith is a fifteen-year Army veteran who served during and after Desert Storm. He has an MA in English and is currently pursuing an MFA in poetry from the University of Massachusetts–Boston. He is a father of five and a grandfather. He currently resides in Cambridge, MA, with his wife.

Lisa Stice is a poet/mother/military spouse. She is the author of two full-length collections, *Permanent Change of Station* (Middle West Press, 2018) and *Uniform* (Aldrich Press, 2016), and a chapbook, *Desert* (Prolific Press). While it is difficult to say where home is, she currently lives in North Carolina with her husband, daughter, and dog. You can learn more about her and her publications at lisastice.wordpress.com and at facebook.com/LisaSticePoet.

Ryan Stovall is a former adventurer, world traveler, and Green Beret. His poetry won the 2018 Wright Award from Line of Advance, and has appeared in *The Deadly Writer's Patrol, Rosebud, The Cape Rock, Here Comes Everyone*, and other journals. Ryan lives with his family near Bangor, Maine.

Mary Ellen Talley's poems have recently been published in *Raven Chronicles, U City Review*, and *Ekphrastic Review*, as well as in anthologies, *All We Can Hold* and *Ice Cream Poems*. Her poetry has received two Pushcart nominations. Her sister's husband served in Vietnam, helicoptering wounded and dead. Her husband served state-side 1970–1972. Her daughter is married to a Navy submariner.

Major A. Sean Taylor enlisted in the Iowa Army National Guard on October 24, 2002, at the age of 35. He deployed to Bagram, Afghanistan, with the Iowa Guard from 2010–2011 and to Taji, Iraq, with the U.S. Army Reserve in 2015, supporting Iraqi Security Forces with their fight against ISIS.

Jonathan Tennis is a graduate of Eckerd College (BA), Norwich University (MSIA), and the University of Tampa (MFA). After serving in the U.S. Army, he moved to Tampa, where he still resides and works as a consultant. His writing has appeared in the *Eckerd Review, Military Experience and the Arts, 0-Dark-Thirty, Odet, Proud to Be: Writing by American Warriors, Sanctuary Literary and Arts Journal*, and a festschrift in honor of the poet Peter Meinke.

George Uriah served in the U.S. Army from 1996–2001, primarily at Fort Carson, Colorado, with a deployment to Bosnia. He completed an undergraduate degree from Vanderbilt University and a Master's in history from the University of Tennessee. In 2006, two short stories of his appeared in *Thin Air Magazine* and the *Timber Creek Review*. He lives in Nashville with a border collie.

Aaron Wallace is a veteran poet who served and deployed as a combat medic in the 3rd Infantry Division during Operation Iraqi Freedom. Since Aaron's discharge in 2013, he has graduated from Jacksonville University with Honors and is a current member of Lesley University's Master of Fine Arts program. His work has been published in *The Wrath-Bearing Tree, The Deadly Writers Patrol*, and is forthcoming in *North Dakota Quarterly*. Aaron currently resides in Jacksonville, Florida, with his wonderful wife Darby and their dogs, Bailey and Benji.

William J. Watkins Jr. is a veteran of the U.S. Army (1988–1991). He served in the 302nd MI Battalion, which was attached to V Corps. His short stories have appeared in various publications such as *Forge Journal, Moon Magazine, Foliate Oak, The Opening Line, Bangalore Review*, and *Corner Club Press*. He has also published three books of non-fiction: *Reclaiming the American Revolution* (Palgrave, 2004), *Judicial Monarchs* (McFarland, 2012), and *Patent Trolls* (Independent Institute, 2014). His articles have appeared in various publications including *USA Today, The Washington Times*, and *Forbes*. He is an Assistant U.S. Attorney prosecuting white collar crime.

Valerie Elizabeth Young is a veteran of the United States Armed Forces. She served approximately ten years, with a deployment to Iraq and Hurricane Katrina. She is a Head Start advocate and parent ambassador. As a parent ambassador, she works with other Head Start parents to advocate for Head Start in the state of Illinois. She now also works with the Missouri Department of Corrections as a Probation and Parole Assistant.

Judges Bios

Photography judge **Randy Brown** is a former editor of community and metro newspapers, as well as national trade and consumer magazines. He is now a freelance writer based in Central Iowa. He writes about citizen-soldier culture at www.redbullrising.com, about 21st century war poetry at www.fobhaiku.com, and about military-themed writing at www.aimingcircle.com. Brown is the author of the award-winning poetry collection *Welcome to FOB Haiku: War Poems from Inside the Wire* (2015), and the editor of the non-fiction title *Reporting for Duty: U.S. Citizen-Soldier Journalism from the Afghan Surge, 2010–2011* (2016). The latter involved the curation of more than 360 black-and-white photos. Brown is the current poetry editor at the literary journal *As You Were*, published twice a year by the non-profit Military Experience & the Arts. He is also a member of Military Reporters & Editors, the Military Writers Guild, and the Military Writers Society of America.

Essays judge **Glenn Ferdman**, Director of the Beaverton City Library, is a native of Chicago and earned his Master's degree in Library Science from Indiana University. He has more than 25 years of experience leading and managing public, academic, school, healthcare, and law libraries in Chicago, Kansas City, Boston, and Portland. He is the proud father of three children and enjoys hiking, biking, and swimming in his spare time.

Allison Joseph directs the MFA Program in Creative Writing at Southern Illinois University and also serves as poetry editor of *Crab Orchard Review*, the publisher of No Chair Press, and the director of Writers In Common writing conference. She has published poetry, fiction, chapbooks, nonfiction, and is the author of eight books of poetry, including her latest full-length book of poetry, *Confessions of a Barefaced Woman*, published by Red Hen Press in 2018; another book is upcoming from Red Hen. *Confessions of a Barefaced Woman* was a 2019 nominee in the poetry category of the NAACP Image Awards, has won several national awards, and is a finalist for the Montaigne Medal and the Da Vinci Eye Book Award.

Fiction judge **J. A. Moad II** is a former Air Force C-130 pilot with over a hundred combat sorties. He served as an English professor at the United States Air Force Academy and continues to serve as an editor and blogger for their international journal, *War, Literature & the Arts*. His short stories, poetry, and essays have appeared in a variety of journals and anthologies, and he is the recipient of the *Consequence Magazine* Fiction Award. In addition to writing, he has performed on stage at the Library of Congress and at The Guthrie Theater as part of *The Telling Project—Giving Voice to the Veteran Experience*. His award-winning play, *Outside Paducah—The Wars at Home*, had its New York debut at the Wild Project Theater in 2017, where he was nominated for Outstanding Solo Performance by the New York Innovative Theater Awards. He currently resides in Northfield, MN, and flies for Delta Airlines.